His lips were warm, but cruel.

He paid no attention to her struggles in the steel circle of his arms. Against her, his body was lean and unyielding. It was a deliberate punishment for being less than he had expected her to be. After her first panic, Elizabeth realized in shame he had reason for his action. She herself had disillusioned him and then taunted him with it. She had entered his home under false pretenses, accepted the legacy, in theory at least, that did not belong to her. Regardless of her motives, she could not deny her guilt. She ceased to resist him.

Slowly, almost imperceptibly, a treacherous tenderness crept into the kiss.

Also by Jennifer Blake

THE SECRET OF MIRROR HOUSE

STRANGER AT PLANTATION INN

BRIDE OF A STRANGER

THE NOTORIOUS ANGEL

NIGHT OF THE CANDLES

SWEET PIRACY

THE STORM AND THE SPLENDOR

GOLDEN FANCY

EMBRACE AND CONQUER

ROYAL SEDUCTION

SURRENDER IN MOONLIGHT

TENDER BETRAYAL

MIDNIGHT WALTZ

FIERCE EDEN

ROYAL PASSION

PRISONER OF DESIRE

SOUTHERN RAPTURE

LOUISIANA DAWN

PERFUME OF PARADISE

Dark Masquerade

by
Jennifer Blake

This first hardcover edition published in Great Britain 1990 by
SEVERN HOUSE PUBLISHERS LTD of
35 Manor Road, Wallington, Surrey SM6 0BW
with acknowledgement to Ballantine Books, a
division of Random House, Inc., New York

First U.S.A. hardcover edition published 1990 by
SEVERN HOUSE PUBLISHERS INC, NEW YORK

Blake, Jennifer, *1942*–
  Dark Masquerade
  I. Title
  823'.914 [F]

  ISBN 0-7278-4039-8

Distributed in the U.S.A. by
Mercedes Distribution Center, Inc.
62 Imlay Street, Brooklyn, N.Y. 11231

Printed and bound in Great Britain
at the University Press, Cambridge

To my children, Ronnie, Ricky, Lindy, and Kathy

CHAPTER 1

The evening sun hovered over the tops of the trees. Its orange shafts struck through the dark woods, harrying the coach as it swayed along, gleaming on its brass fittings and the cracked blue paint on its sides. The sun's rays were still bright but they had lost their heat. A damp coolness seemed to seep from the encroaching trees and undergrowth, and the muddy water, thrown up as the wheels jolted through the potholes in the road, had a chill, dank smell.

The driver on the box resettled his hat, pulling the brim lower to shield his eyes, and then he took up his blacksnake whip and sent it cracking over the horses' heads as he yelled curses at the leaders. The coach picked up speed.

At the windows the dirty brown leather curtains bellied and slapped, doing little to stop the muddy water that spattered in and trickled down the sides. The doors rattled loosely in their frames and the body creaked as it swung on its straps, while above the rumbling of the wheels and the pounding of the horses' hooves the bumping of a loose trunk could be heard.

The man on the forward seat, a merchant judging from his false shirt front, old fashioned stock, and self-satisfied air, threw back his head and glared upward.

Beside him his wife misunderstood. "That man will kill us all," she said, with an accusing look at the girl on the opposite seat. "I'm surprised we haven't overturned a dozen times already!" The woman's eyes were protuberant and her mouth colorless. The grayish brown hair skewered in a knot on top of her head was pulled too tight, dragging her heavy brows upward in a look of constant surprise.

"Sounds like we be about to lose that lot of gee-gaws I've got overhead. Happen I'll have to charge somebody with 'em, if they turn up missing." The merchant eyed the girl also. When she made no answer he pushed the window curtain aside with one long finger, and holding back his chin whiskers, let fly a stream of tobacco juice. It was a comment.

Two small tow-headed boys, their hair like cropped white silk, sat on the middle seat, a plain wooden board. With their arms hooked over the wide leather strap that served as a back rest, they turned guileless blue eyes on the girl to see if she had taken their father's point.

If she had, Mary Elizabeth Brewster gave no indication. Her deep green eyes were fixed on a point above the heads of the merchant and his wife while she drew the strings of her black reticule through her fingers. She had no liking for the merchant and his wife, but after forty long miles spent that day in their company she could understand their annoyance. Not only were they riding with their backs to the horses, but they were being taken some fourteen miles out of their way. It could not be helped. Callie could not be the one to ride backward, because she turned queasy riding backward. As for the detour, that was the chance they took when they boarded public transportation.

Above them the driver swung his whip in a series of sharp reports. Elizabeth lifted a speculative glance. Perhaps a silver dollar had been too much to offer the man on the box for this side trip. It had been Mexican to be sure, but coins were so scarce these days. She appreciated his efforts to get a little more speed out of the lumbering old coach, although it was anybody's guess whether it was the thought of making up his schedule which drove him, or, as was more likely, the thought of the drunk possible on his windfall, with whiskey at a quarter per gallon.

It doesn't matter, she told herself fiercely. What mattered was that she and Callie and the baby got to Oak Shade with as little delay as possible.

Beside her, Callie, her name the inevitable shortening from Calliope, the muse of the soft voice, sat as stolid and immovable as a mountain. In her ample lap the baby slept. When Elizabeth looked down at him, her mouth curved unconsciously into a smile. Such a good baby. Their nine days on this bone-wracking trip over a part of Texas and most of Louisiana would have been very different if he had not been a good traveler. As it was, it had been an endurance test. For the first three or four days they had felt bruised and battered as if they had been beaten. But for the last five they had been so mindlessly weary that they had almost ceased to feel; almost, but not quite. The muscles in Elizabeth's arms ached from holding the baby mile after mile, spelling Callie. Though she never complained, the Negro nurse must be even more tired. On her shoulders had fallen the main burden of caring for little Joseph, not only in the coach but in the primitive taverns and sleazy inns that had provided overnight accommodation. Callie was good with babies as well as being a wonderful wet nurse. The stillborn deaths of six of her own babies, the last only two weeks before Joseph's birth, had given her a need and a love for the feel of a child in her arms.

Soberly Elizabeth pleated the black bombazine of her dress without really seeing the nervous reaction of her fingers. Even in repose, however, the pale oval of her face did not lose the look of determination about the mouth and chin that had unconsciously alienated the merchant and his wife. Her emerald eyes, heavily lashed beneath dark arched brows, gave no hint of her inner conflict.

Without Callie, Elizabeth thought, this journey, this masquerade would never have been undertaken. For a moment the thought of what she intended to do sent a shudder of dread over her. Her reasons for what she was doing, so carefully thought out, so important, had fled, and she was left with the feeling that she was being incredibly foolhardy, that she would be found out in the first minutes of meeting the family at Oak Shade. *Turn back,* a part of her mind cried, and she had to clench her jaws together to keep from giving the order.

Then beside her the baby, Joseph, stirred, waving a plump fist in the air. He smiled in his sleep. Her doubts fell away. No, the consequences of not going through with this masquerade were too great. Besides, it was too late to turn back now. It had been too late from the day she had placed a wooden marker on the fresh grave which lay beneath a cottonwood tree by a rambling log house in Texas. A marker bearing her own name.

Strangely, the thought of the marker gave her a feeling of relief. She had made her choice weeks before. There could be no turning back. All that was needed was a little resolution. There was so much to be gained and so little to lose.

She let her eyes rest for a moment on the merchant and his wife and children. Their bright examining eyes had evaluated her from the gold band on her left hand to the mourning brooch made of hair at her throat, from the black high-button shoes peeping from beneath her skirts to the bright auburn hair drawn back in a knot at the nape of her neck and covered by her semi-transparent mourning veil. She had deceived them. It could be done again.

A mirthless smile touched her generous mouth. How shocked they would be if they knew that, despite her widow's weeds and the baby in the arms of his Negro nurse, she had never had a husband, never been a mother, and from this day would answer to a dead woman's name.

"Whoa, whoa!"

The shout was followed by the grinding of brakes. The coach began to slow and finally came to a lurching stop.

"What can it be?" The merchant's wife clutched her husband's arm.

He shook her off and twitched the leather curtain aside.

"Some fancy landau seems to have blocked the road. Nabob's rig, no doubt. Got a black in livery at the ribbons."

Outside, the servant in the carriage could be heard asking for a Madame Delacroix. With a start Elizabeth realized he meant her, but she made no move to alight and sternly repressed an impulse to lean across and peep out around the slack curtain. In a moment the driver climbed down and pulled open the door.

"Mrs. Delacroix, ma'am, this feller says he has orders to carry y'all the rest of the way."

"Thank you," Elizabeth replied with the quiet dignity befitting a recent widow.

Turning to Callie, she took the baby while Callie clambered out, and then gave him back into her keeping while she herself accepted the driver's hand and stepped down.

In a few minutes they had been handed into the landau and their trunks and boxes lashed on behind. With a jerk, they started off, leaving the coach behind them to the difficult business of turning on the narrow road.

Elizabeth threw the veil away from her face, drawing its long length across one shoulder to prevent it from being crushed beneath her, and then pushed her skirts into place around her feet.

"We forgot to say good-by," she told Callie, frowning.

"So did they," Callie answered without looking up from the baby who had been awakened by the move.

The landau was well sprung, and it had deeply padded seats and gray velvet upholstery. It seemed luxurious in comparison to the stage, whose hard seats and body swung on straps gave no protection from the jolts. It was an open carriage, however, and the damp dew-laden chill of the gathering dusk made Elizabeth shiver and Callie draw Joseph closer against her breasts.

But this last stage of their journey was not a long one, and soon they were turning into a long winding drive. It was lined with evergreen live oaks that acted as a dust screen, the oaks that gave the house its name. Elizabeth felt their dark shade drop over them as they swept under their arching branches up the drive. She was aware of a sudden depression, and her earlier apprehension swept back in force. The sound of the carriage was loud in the soft black stillness. Through the trees, rows of white pillars gleamed, fleeting and ethereal. Then suddenly the carriage broke from the shade, and the house, like a Grecian temple in a forest, was before them. Insubstantial in the dusky darkness, it seemed cold, distant and forbidding. A flame, like a votive candle, flickered in the wrought iron lantern hanging over the front door, but there was no other sign of life. A desolation that was near to tears closed over Elizabeth at this lack of welcome. Suppose it

11

had been Ellen Marie arriving, gentle, easily hurt Ellen Marie, her sister whose place she was taking?

"Is there no one home?" she asked the driver sharply in an effort to cover her misgivings.

"Oh, yes'm. They home alright. I expect they at the supper table."

She waited while he wrapped the reins around the whip in its stand and climbed down to come around and hand her out of the carriage. She stepped down and waited until Callie struggled out with the sleeping baby. Then Elizabeth swept up the steps, her long black veil swirling about her knees. With one hand clutching her reticule and the other holding her skirts out of the way, she crossed the brick-floored gallery, Callie hurrying behind as though afraid to lose sight of her.

As she neared the front door, it swung wide and a white-coated Negro butler bowed low and then stepped back for her to enter. She glanced at him inquiringly but he had the impassive countenance of all good servants. In the great central hall she stopped.

The hall stretching through the center of the house was floored with polished squares of black and white marble. Against the right wall stood a massive table with a white marble top and the curved cabriole legs of a Chippendale piece. Upon it sat a silver tray for visiting cards and a heavy glass lamp. The lamp had an elaborate base of small stylized glass dragons, a dark green globe that nearly concealed the flickering flame within, and crystal lusters that tinkled faintly in the draft from the open door. Behind the table the wall was covered with an oriental wall-paper in celadon green with a pattern of drooping weeping willows and pensive, small-faced, slant-eyed maidens.

To the left rose a wide staircase with a mahogany stair rail ending at the foot of the stairs in a serpentine coil that served as a newel post. In the center of the coil was fixed a smooth ivory button, a symbol that the house was paid for, that it carried no mortgage.

Seeing her hesitation, the butler bowed again and begged her to step into the library. Though she had the curious feeling that she was being maneuvered, Elizabeth had no choice but to comply. It was only after she was in the library that it occurred to her that as member of the family she should have been shown into the front parlor, or salon as the Creoles called it, instead of this lesser room.

After holding a spill to the lamp in the hall, the butler lit several lamps for them in the library, saw that they were seated and then went away.

Minutes passed. Elizabeth and Callie were too tired to speak, and the ticking of the ormolu clock on the white Carrara marble mantle over the fireplace was loud in the silence. Callie sighed, shifted in her chair, and patted Joseph, who was hungrily trying to suck his fist. Elizabeth got to her feet and paced, looking at the somber elegance of the room. Burgundy velvet drapes, heavily fringed with gold tassels, hung over the Swiss lace panels at the windows. A gold rug with a border of swirling green leaves covered the floor, and the walnut settee and chairs were covered with red brocatelle picked out with gold thread. The faint odor of tobacco hung on the air, coming she discovered from a humidor on one of the small tables sitting about the room. There was also a smell of leather which came from the books that lined the walls and from the large leather chair that stood behind a heavy desk that took up the far end of the long room. The two smells combined to give an impression of masculinity to the room.

Abruptly the door swung open and the butler stood back to allow a man to enter. Elizabeth turned to face him and made a move to step forward then checked herself. No, let him come to her, she thought. It would not do to appear too eager. But as the man came toward her she found herself wondering if it would not have been easier to go to him than to sustain that dark and searching regard.

A black armband was fastened over the sleeve of his deep gray frock coat. Beneath the coat he wore a black embroidered waistcoat with fawn pantaloons. Onyx shirt studs gleamed against the white of his pleated and tucked shirt front and at his collar a pure white cravat contrasted with the deep sun bronze of his face. His dark hair was brushed back severely over his ears, and the fine curl threatening to fall from the brush pattern lent no note of softness to the black gaze of his eyes.

"You will be my brother's wife. I bid you welcome to Oak Shade," he said with a slight bow.

As she gave him her hand he carried it to his lips. The action was so unexpected that Elizabeth flinched, and then tried to recover the slip by smiling quickly and thanking him. But he had not overlooked her reaction, and an added stiffness came into his manner.

"And you must be Bernard," she said brightly, trying to overcome her nervousness. "Felix spoke of you often. I must thank you for sending the carriage to meet us."

"Not at all. I am told my driver could not bring you the entire distance from town. I am sorry. It was most remiss of him, especially since he has met every coach from the north for the past three days. I would not want you to find our hospitality lacking."

"It was my fault. I had the driver bypass the town to come straight here. It seemed best. I didn't realize that you would send the carriage for us since I didn't, in my letter, give you any real idea of when we would be arriving. I had no very real idea myself."

"In the future you will find it best perhaps to leave such arrangements in my hands."

"I'm—sure I shall," Elizabeth murmured, noting his obvious disapproval of what she had done, but resolving to maintain her independence. Something about his manner set her teeth on edge, and she found her smile fading until they were staring at each other in near hostility. There was an exactness about him that she did not like, from the precise folds of his cravat and the perfect set of his coat across the shoulders, to the trim of his fashionably long sideburns. There was a chiseled appearance to the planes of his face, in the high cheek bones, firm chin, and the contours of his mouth. Thick black brows divided by two parallel grooves, as of constant anger or irritation, gave him a forbidding look. There had been a faint French accent in his speech that might have been attractive if his voice had not been so cold. The only thing about him that she could approve was that he was clean shaven, though

14

this was a mark of a strong, near arrogant, self-confidence in a hirsute decade.

Callie sighed heavily again, and for the first time, Bernard Delacroix seemed to notice the Negro woman and the fretting baby she held. He stared at Joseph for a long moment, so long that Elizabeth said, "The child is tired and hungry, that is all."

He brought his gaze back to her face. "Yes, of course. You must all be tired. If you will be seated I will have someone show you to your room."

He had hardly finished speaking before the door opened once again and the butler bowed a plump middle-aged woman into the room.

"What is this, Bernard?" she said, a glint of avid curiosity in her small black eyes. "Why have you left the supper table? Who are these people?"

"This lady," he answered her with a stress on the second word as a reproof, "is my brother's wife, the mother of his child."

An alarming wave of color rose in the florid face of the older woman. "That's impossible," she snapped, "Felix has been dead very nearly a year."

"I assure you it is so." There was a stern note in his voice that did not fail to reach her. She looked long and measuringly at the baby, who was fast becoming furious as his hunger rose.

"How old?" she asked abruptly of Elizabeth. The woman spoke in the Creole French of the area, as had Bernard when he answered her. Bernard made a move to translate but Elizabeth forestalled him. "I understand."

Her mother had been born and reared in New Orleans. Her mother had met her father, a Mississippi planter, while visiting relatives in Natchez.

To the woman she said in a cool voice, "Joseph is four months old."

Bernard Delacroix did not lack a sense of humor. "Let me present you," he said dryly, "to my step-mother, Madame Alma Delacroix."

The older woman barely acknowledged the introduction. With her small plump hands folded across the silk of her black dress she demanded, "Why wasn't I told?"

Bernard began to answer her, but as it was nearly impossible to be heard above the now crying baby, he did not continue. He turned toward the door, looking, Elizabeth supposed, for the butler to summon assistance. When he saw who stood in the doorway a faint smile touched his lips.

"Grand'mere," he said, "what kept you?"

A white-haired woman with steel spectacles on her nose and a cane in her hand advanced into the room. Dressed in black from the pointed leather shoes on her feet to the batiste cap trimmed with black ribbon on her high-held head, she was actually smiling as she came toward Elizabeth.

"You there," she said to Callie, ignoring Bernard's comment. "Take my great-grandson and follow that girl." She jerked her head toward a Negro maid in a white cap and apron who was hovering in the doorway. "Mind you be careful of him going up the stairs. Ask the girl for whatever you need to make him comfortable, but hurry. I dislike intensely to hear a baby crying!"

Elizabeth helped Callie to her feet with a hand under her elbow. Then she watched in some trepidation as they left the room.

"You may be easy," Grand'mere said calmly. "They will be cared for, I assure you."

"Yes, of course," Elizabeth replied, summoning a smile.

"I believe it will be best if you also seek your bed. Quite frankly, you appear exhausted."

She glanced at her grandson. "You agree, Bernard? I think all discussion can be postponed until tomorrow. We have waited this long, a few hours more will make no difference. In any event, if we delay here very much longer we will have Darcourt and Celestine with us."

Bernard inclined his head but made no move to go, his eyes narrow as he gazed at Elizabeth's pale face.

"Sherry and biscuits usually make our supper since we have a large mid-day meal, but I will have something a little more substantial sent to you shortly."

"I would be grateful."

Alma Delacroix had been listening impatiently.

"You will oblige me, Bernard—unless of course, you *wish* to hold a family conclave?"

Bernard stared at her a moment, and then lowered his eyelids. With a slight shake of his head, he offered his arm to the plump woman, his step-mother, and led her from the room, her neck craning back over her shoulder.

For a long time after they had gone the old lady they called Grand'mere stared at Elizabeth. "You have a good chin," she said at last. "And you seem like a sensible girl, not quite what I expected, but sensible. That is an exceedingly rare quality here at Oak Shade. You would do well to cultivate it." Her old voice held a dry humor. Then a stiffness came into her manner.

"I believe in plain speaking and I want you to believe that what I am about to say is to help you make some sort of life here with us. You cannot help but be aware that your marriage to my grandson Felix was a surprise to his family, an unpleasant surprise. He had been betrothed to his cousin, Celestine, since they were children. The betrothal is a serious matter to us Creoles. We are the foreign born descendants of pure French and Spanish forebears and follow their strict marital traditions. The betrothal is an alliance, a contract signed by all parties. To a Creole, breaking off the betrothal is almost as unheard of as breaking the marriage! You must understand our feelings. Felix's death in the war in Texas was not only a great sorrow to us all, but it was also unfortunate for you since you will not have his love and support to help you become a part of this family."

She looked up at Elizabeth to see how she was affected by that statement, and seeing no sign of tears, went on: "You must know that you have been asked to come here for the sake of Felix's son. Perhaps I should not speak of it, but I dislike pretense. I do not know why you have accepted my invitation, I only know that I am glad you have. It required courage, I'm sure. I will do what I can to help you make a place for yourself among us, but you must expect a certain amount of resentment. It is not unnatural under the circumstances."

"I understand," Elizabeth said quietly when she saw that the old lady had finished. A quiet anger seethed in her mind, and she found herself once again feeling nearly glad that it was herself and not Ellen who was here. She understood perfectly. She understood that she was on trial, that if there were adjustments to be made in order for her to live at Oak Shade, she would be expected to make them. She would have to learn to accommodate her life to theirs. She must not be offended because they did not want her but only Joseph. She was to be accepted for his sake. Unconsciously she raised her head. Very well. Their attitude made no difference. She had come, after all, for Joseph's sake also. Joseph had a rightful place here at Oak Shade plantation. So long as he was accepted, loved and cared for, she did not care whether she belonged or not, if she could be with him. Their affection was not necessary for her welfare.

"There is one other thing you should realize. Celestine, the girl Felix was to marry, is living here in the house. Her parents are touring in France, a protracted visit to relatives. For the time being Bernard and I are acting as her guardians. Perhaps you will remember that she is our cousin and try to understand her position. She regards herself in the light of a widow. She loved Felix, you know, and has been in deepest mourning for him."

Elizabeth felt a flush of indignation mounting to her cheeks, but there seemed little to say. How would she have felt, she wondered, if she had in truth been Felix's widow? How could she have brought herself to stay in this house in circumstances like these? It was a useless question. She knew very well that if she had had any legal claim to her sister's child, she would never have come at all.

"Come," the old lady said imperiously. "Give me your arm up the stairs. If I keep you here much longer Bernard will wonder why he should not have his discussion with you also."

"Perhaps he should," Elizabeth said in a tight voice.

"I forbid it. You are much too fatigued. It would not be at all the thing."

Elizabeth's antagonism began to fade as they slowly climbed the stairs. As she held the old lady's elbow she could feel the fragile bones and sense a faint but constant trembling. But though her anger was gone, a depression

18

remained. It settled deeper over her when she glanced over the banister rail and caught sight of the family at the supper table. The room below was bright with a dozen candles. There were candles in the twin candelabra on the sideboard and in the chandelier above the table. An *epergne* filled to overflowing with white azaleas sat in the center of the white lace cloth which was studded with silver and crystal. Bernard and his step-mother had returned to their places at the table, and there was also a young woman at the board who she thought must be Celestine. She was dressed in black, though her mourning was relieved by a pink camellia at the neckline of the lace bertha that fell over the great, drooping puff sleeves of her dress. Another flower nestled atop the curls of soft black hair at the back of her head, which were drawn back from a demure center part. Her finely molded face was tinted with delicate color as she toyed with a small wine glass and laughed across the table at Bernard. A second man sat at the table, but though he was somberly dressed also, as befitted a house of mourning, his face held a look of such reckless gaiety that Elizabeth came to a halt, startled. His hair gleamed in golden waves under the candlelight and his laughing eyes appeared blue, though it was hard to be certain at such a distance. As she watched he lounged back in his chair, said something to Celestine, and touched a fingertip to his neat mustache, which was a shade darker in color than his hair.

"That is Darcourt, a thorough-going scamp, but likable enough," Grand'mere said, following the direction of her gaze. "My son married twice. Bernard and Felix are of the first marriage, Darcourt and Theresa are the children of the second. Theresa you will see later." There was a shade of contempt in her voice that brought Elizabeth's head around, but the old lady went on as if she was unaware of her interest. "My son has been dead for some time. Perhaps it is a good thing. God does, at times, dispense small mercies."

As they moved on up the stairs Elizabeth looked back. A scamp he might be, but he was undeniably a handsome one. He was more handsome in his way than Bernard, though it might have been his animation, his obvious enjoyment of life, that gave that impression. There was a great contrast between the two men, not only in their coloring, but also in their faces. Where Bernard was sunbronzed Darcourt was pale, and where Bernard's mouth was stern with overly firm lines, the other man's curved with an attractive and faintly sensuous charm.

As they turned the corner around the upper newel post Elizabeth felt oddly reluctant to leave that scene of laughter and comfortable living downstairs. It had been a long time since she had enjoyed either. Deep inside her there was a stirring of longing. She had been a part of a family once. Now she was alone, alone with the responsibility for her small nephew. To belong again, to share the responsibility, to be relieved of worries—the thought was seductive. It was also impossible. Angrily she shook her head, and as she walked on she raised her chin higher in atonement for that moment of weakness.

They passed two small Negro boys scuffling on a long padded bench; these were errand boys stationed in the hall to carry messages and run small errands. Then the two women came to a large bedroom at the front of the house.

Firelight, the only illumination, flickered redly on the hearth, leaving the rest of the room in shadow. Beside the fire a pan of water sat, left from Joseph's bath, and near it Callie sat rocking slowly back and forth. The sleeping child, clean and replete, lay against her shoulder. His dark hair curled in wispy fineness over his head and his long lashes lay on his plump cheeks. His great-grandmother stood looking down at him, and then she turned away, her face impassive.

At their entrance the figure of a woman glided from the depths of darkness near the great four-poster bed. Her skirts of black taffeta made a whispering rustle and the small gold earrings in her ears caught the yellow gleam of the fire. Obviously a French lady's maid, she could have been any age from twenty-five to forty. Her narrow eyes skimmed over Elizabeth's serviceable but unmodish mourning clothes and dismissed them with a tiny derisive movement of her thin lips. She bowed her elaborately dressed head to Grand'mere and set her pale face into deliberately pleasant lines.

"Madame is ready to prepare for bed? If these intruders can be dismissed I will help her. I was certain my mistress could not have ordered this woman and her charge to come here, to her own room, but I could not make this stupid girl who calls herself a house servant attend me, and I would never disturb Madame at supper."

"Do not fuss, Denise," Grand'mere said absently. "I must think."

"But Madame—"

"Be still, I say."

A silence alive with the offended dignity of the maid, Denise, descended.

Suddenly Grand'mere spoke. "The child must sleep in here with me, of course. This room is one of the largest in the house. His nurse will be able to stay near him at night, and since you, Ellen Marie, will wish to be nearby also, you must have the room beside me. It has a connecting door. Denise sleeps there in the ordinary way, but she can very well have another room, perhaps the one next to the nursery." The old lady seemed not to hear Denise's gasp of outrage.

"There is no need for that," Elizabeth protested, aware of the maid's inimical glance toward her. "If there is a nursery—"

"There is every need. No child in this family has ever gone to the nursery until he was three at least. It is much safer to have your babies near you. I always did."

Elizabeth acquiesced, but she thought uncomfortably that it would not make her position any easier to have the household routine disrupted on her account. Then she smiled to herself as she realized that it would not be for her at all but for Joseph.

She stood back as orders were issued and the errand boys in the hall were sent scurrying with instructions. In a very short time a cradle and a trundle bed had been set up in the room, and a light supper had been spread on a table before the fire. The room next door was swept clean of the maid's possessions, the bed remade, and her own trunks brought up and unpacked. Then a long Julep tub was brought up and placed near the fireplace. It was filled with hot water from a can brought with half-running footsteps and a great deal of subdued giggling from the servant girls. Tactfully Grand'mere went back downstairs, taking Callie with her to have her own meal in the kitchen.

The rest of the family might have had sherry and biscuits for supper, but for Elizabeth the kitchen had conjured up breast of chicken served on a bed of rice with a piquant sauce, new potatoes in their jackets, fresh peas, and for dessert, strawberries with cream over a sponge cake, and an excellent madeira. It was delicious, but Elizabeth hurried through it. She was spurred by the thought of the hot bath waiting, her first since leaving Texas nearly a week and a half before.

She stepped into the tub and lay soaking, feeling the tiredness, the soreness, melting away. The feel of the water was silky against her skin and the pleasant tang of the lavender soap imported from England gave her a feeling of luxurious comfort. It had been some time since scented soap had been a part of her life.

A length of toweling lay on a slipper chair standing between the fireplace and the tub. Elizabeth reached out and dragged the chair away from the fire. She could smell the odor of hot lacquer; the chair was much too good to allow its finish to be blistered from the heat. The other furnishings in the room were equally good. An enormous four-poster bed of dark wood with a green canopy and hangings stood against one wall. The cradle at the foot was an exact replica of the larger bed, even to the mosquito netting that was looped inside the canopy. A rosewood washstand and a giant armoire, reaching within inches of the high ceiling, were companion pieces to the bed. But the *prie-dieu* in the corner had a different look, a Spanish appearance, with its carved rest and padded leather bench. It reminded Elizabeth of the altar at the Spanish mission where Ellen and Felix had knelt, of the sonorous words of the marriage service spoken by the priest, the flickering candles and the heavy scent of flowers and wafted incense. Connected as it was with their deaths, however, it was not a happy memory. Elizabeth shook her head to banish it, but there was no escape. The black crepe of deep mourning hanging over the pictures on the walls, on the mirrors, and even surmounting the windows, was a glaring reminder.

She frowned and stood up suddenly, sloshing the bath water over onto the floor. Exclaiming in annoyance, she reached for the towel and stepped out of the tub, and then she went still as a strange noise came from the connecting room. Unlike the bustle of preparation that had been going on earlier, this had a furtive sound. As she listened it came again, the rustling of cloth or bed covers, and then there was the scrape of a hasty footstep and a muffled thump as the door into the hall was softly closed.

A servant returning to finish some small forgotten job, she tried to tell herself as she hurriedly skimmed into her night gown and pulled her dressing gown around her. But somehow she could not make herself believe it. A silence had fallen over the house. It had been some time since she had seen the family at the dinner table. Where were they now? Had they come up to bed? She glanced over her shoulder at Joseph sleeping quietly in the cradle. Assured that he was safe, she jerked the belt of her dressing gown in a knot and then walked to the connecting door, turned the knob, and pushed it open.

There was no one there, but then she had not expected there to be, remembering the sound of the closing door. The room was neat, orderly, and apparently unchanged from the way the maids had left it. Or was it? Hadn't the bed been left turned for the night? But why come back in and make it up again?

The bed looked soft, tempting with its feather mattress and spread of muslin edged with lace. The thought of all the lumpy, smelly mattresses she had endured in the past week came to her, and she felt an almost unendurable weariness. It might be diplomatic, and better-mannered, to wait up to bid her hostess good-night, but she did not know where the old lady had gone or when she would return. The warm fire and the hot bath had made leaden weights of her eyelids, relaxed knotted muscles, and taken the last vestige of her energy.

Slowly she moved forward, caught the spread, and flung it back.

Suddenly she jerked her hand away, a surprised cry catching in her throat. Between the bed pillows of the four-poster bed lay a green preserving jar. Its loose glass lid had fallen open as the spread was removed, and spiders, released from their prison, crawled from the jar, spreading out over the sheet.

Small and large, brown and gray, a dozen or more spiders ran or crept in all directions, their legs casting multiplying shadows in the light of the candle beside the bed. Then over the glass lid a last spider came crawling. Its plump, unwieldy body was a shining black, and on the underside an orange hourglass could just barely be seen.

A black widow!

·CHAPTER 2

Disbelief gripped her and she stood staring. Was it some kind of macabre joke? A black widow for a widow in black? Then as a shiver of revulsion rippled over her skin she whipped around and scooped up a wooden handled hairbrush from the washstand. Though she had to lean over the other creeping insects to get to it, she crushed the black widow first, grinding it into the sheet, and then with an anger approaching hysteria she flailed at the others, smashing them with the back of the hairbrush while her hair swung around her face.

"My dear girl, what are you doing?"

With clenched teeth Elizabeth ran down a spider escaping under the fold of the bedspread before she turned.

"Killing spiders!" she said fiercely to the old lady standing in the door. With the back of one hand she pushed her damp hair out of her eyes. "Spiders that someone put in my bed!"

The old lady clutched the door frame, the gaze of her

faded brown eyes going to the glass jar nestled between the pillows of the bed. "Spiders?" she echoed.

Then with an effort she seemed to collect herself, though as she came into the room she leaned heavily on the ebony cane in her hand. She reached for the corner of the mattress, tugging at the sheets, but at her action, Callie, who had slipped into the room behind Grand'mere, took the bedclothes from her hand and silently began to strip the bed, folding the corners toward the center to hold any live insects.

"I must get someone up here to sweep down the rails of the bed—" the old lady said to herself vaguely. "No—that will not do, it will be all over the house in a trice." Without appearing to realize she was speaking aloud she stared hard at Callie. "Give me the jar."

When she complied, Grand'mere tucked the jar under her arm and turned to Elizabeth. "I would offer you another room, but there is none. There are only eight bedrooms above stairs, counting the little one off the nursery that Denise is occupying. Perhaps if you and your woman inspected this one thoroughly you would feel comfortable enough to sleep here?"

"I—suppose so," Elizabeth answered, unable to keep her reluctance from her voice.

Grand'mere hesitated. "You may have my bed and I shall sleep in here then."

But Elizabeth had not missed the hesitation or the older woman's reluctance to enter the room.

"Oh no. You must not think of it. I—I am persuaded that once we have looked it over carefully, I will be able to sleep easily."

"You are sure?"

"Quite sure."

Elizabeth wanted to smile at this polite exchange but did not. Looking down, she saw that her hands were still trembling.

Together she and Callie swept the bed railings, brushed the canopy and shook out the mosquito netting and bed hangings. They beat the mattress and dusted it, and remade the bed with fresh linen smelling of vetiver and a clean bedspread of heavy crochet work. When they were

25

through, Elizabeth was calmer, and so exhausted that she felt she could have slept on the floor.

After blowing out the candle, she lay staring up into the darkness of the canopy, imagining she felt things crawling on her arms and her face. She was fairly certain in her mind that the bed was free of spiders, but she was unable to relax.

Who would do such a thing to her? Had Denise been angry enough at being ousted from her room to take that sort of revenge? But if she had, would she have had time to catch the spiders? No, not unless she had expected to be ousted and had thought to give Elizabeth a disgust of the room so she would refuse to stay in it. But the black widow might have bitten her. Surely Denise, no matter how piqued over the loss of the room, would not go that far?

But who would?

She awoke slowly, coming out of the heavy sleep of exhaustion to find Callie standing beside her bed with a small coffee cup on a tray.

"Here's your eye-opener, Mis' Elizabeth. The old lady said tell you breakfast'll be ready in thirty minutes, but you don't have to get up, if you don't want to. I can send one of the boys in the hall to tell the cook to send it up."

Elizabeth's eyes were grainy and sore and her arms and legs felt weighted. She would have liked to stay in bed, but the inclination to linger was banished as the thought of the spiders slipped into her mind.

"I'll get up," she said, sitting up and carefully taking the coffee cup onto her lap. Then she froze.

"Callie!"

The Negro woman swung around, her dark eyes large in her round face.

"You called me Elizabeth, Callie. Ellen, Miss Ellen. You must remember."

Callie caught her lip between her teeth and looked over her shoulder into the next room. She sighed with relief. "I'm sorry, I truly am. But you so different from your sister."

"Nonsense. We had the same coloring."

26

"Yes'm. But Mis' Ellen's eyes was soft and not so green and her hair was lighter, most nearly blonde 'stead of being dark ginger. And she was kinda helpless and didn't know how to go about things."

Elizabeth put one hand to her eyes. "Yes, I know what you mean, but you must try to remember. You must!"

"Yes'm, you can count on me. I won't forget again, especially when there's anybody around."

"It doesn't matter whether anyone is around or not, Callie. You can never tell when someone may be listening. They don't want us here, you and I. One of them put those spiders in this bed last night."

"Yes'm, I know that, and mean and spiteful is what I call it. We gonna stay on here with such goings-on?"

"We must, Callie. This is where Joseph belongs. A part of it is his. He can have so much here, and I can give him nothing."

"You could leave him here."

Elizabeth smiled at her. They had been through so much together. She knew Callie did not mean what she said; she would be the last to want to leave Joseph. The suggestion was Callie's way of helping Elizabeth to clarify her thinking.

"With these strangers?" Elizabeth asked, shaking her head. "No, I could never do that."

When Callie had gone, Elizabeth sat sipping her coffee. If she was different from Ellen, it was not too surprising. When they had trekked from Mississippi to Texas by ox train, Ellen had been sixteen. In Mississippi Ellen had been a belle; her card had always been filled at the balls. The front veranda of their home had been filled with her suitors in the evenings, and she had already received two proposals of marriage. She had hated the thought of leaving their Mississippi plantation to begin again. She had never been able to understand that the land was worked out, that it could no longer support their way of life. Their mother had died of malaria while they were crossing the swamps of Louisiana. Ellen had been ill with it too, and she had never fully recovered.

Elizabeth had been only thirteen, too young to be included in the social merriment, the balls, the soirées, and the house parties. She had taken after her father. She had loved riding along the wagon train, and she had felt some of the same longing for the ever-receding frontier that had driven him. Being young and strong, she had adapted to the new way of life. She had learned to manage the household, direct the slaves, and see to their health and welfare. She had gone to school at the Spanish mission, riding there and back with a Negro groom trailing behind her, until she was sixteen. At that time she had taken over the house, tactfully easing her sister aside, in spite of Ellen's weak and half-hearted efforts.

She had known things were not going well, even before the outbreak of the revolt they were calling the war for Texas Independence. Her father's heart had never been in the struggle to establish a new plantation, especially since he blamed his wife's death on the move and on himself. The privations of the war, her father's contributions to the cause, and the unsettled state of the economy had finished the new plantation, but Elizabeth did not find this out until his death a month after the war ended.

By that time Ellen was a widow expecting a child. There was nothing they could do but stay on at the house and hope that their creditors would not ask them to leave until after the baby was born.

It had been a terrible time, a time of incessant worry and harassment. Ellen, listless and uncaring after Felix's death, was never truly well. Her morning sickness, extreme in any case, never abated. It left her thin and debilitated. Food was scarce. Elizabeth worked the garden all that long summer, trying to save their small hoard of money and to make it last through the fall and winter, when fresh vegetables would not be available. Their livestock, even their saddle horses, were taken away, leaving them stranded. Then one day a slave trader had come. He had lined up their slaves, most of whom had been with the family all their lives, and marched them away in a coffle. It was after he had gone, and after the dust raised by the shuffling feet had settled, that Elizabeth found Callie hiding in the root cellar. Callie was pregnant, and she had known that the long walk would almost surely bring on a miscarriage.

Elizabeth brought her into the house and hid her, but apparently Callie was never missed from the coffle. It was one of the few times that Elizabeth found something to be grateful for in the war. No one expected an accurate accounting of slaves in those confused times.

Then came the months of waiting. Callie's baby had been born dead, possibly from the lack of a doctor's care. On a cold and windy December day two weeks later, Elizabeth had helped Callie to deliver Joseph. It had been a long labor and a difficult one. At the last Ellen had been too weak to help. Her mind had wandered, it had appeared that she imagined herself to be living in that brief spring month when she had first met Felix Delacroix. He had ridden into their homestead for a night's hospitality on his way to join Sam Houston, but then he had stayed to marry her.

Memories washed over Elizabeth as she got out of bed and began to dress, fumbling awkwardly at the buttons at the back of her dress. The memory of blood, so much blood, covering her hands, soaking into the towels and sheets, and draining away her sister's life with it. The memory of fear, and the terrible helplessness, the cold hate for the people who had left them without a way to summon help. And the grave, difficult to dig in the hard, cold earth, so lonely out there where it was exposed to the bitter, sweeping wind.

The buttons done, she turned to the mirror and brushed her hair, twisting it into its usual smooth coil at the nape of her neck. She adjusted the collar of her dress of black fustian and pinned to the neck the mourning brooch Ellen had made from a lock of Felix's hair. Black was not one of her favorite colors, but it was not unbecoming. She wore it gladly, not for Felix, but for her father and for Ellen. To her the color of mourning had become a kind of symbol of what she had been through, and of what was still to be done. She would fight them and their prejudices and pride. Never again did she intend to be as defenseless as she had been in the past year. No, they would not frighten her away with a handful of spiders.

Before leaving the room she checked the door opening into the hall. There was a lock on it but no sign of a key.

Making a mental note to ask Grand'mere for the key, she passed into the other room.

Joseph lay in Callie's lap, cooing and gurgling as the nurse talked to him. Elizabeth leaned over him also, and as she played with him she really saw him as Felix's son for the first time. The blue eyes of the newborn had turned to a brown so dark it was almost black, and the new hair that fuzzed his head was the color of his eyes. He was a stolid baby. He seldom cried unless he was hungry or uncomfortable. It was as if he could sense that all was not quite right with his world.

"Have you eaten, Callie?"

"Oh, yes ma'am. Long ago. The old lady has gone down already. She said you was not to hurry, but I expect maybe you better not keep everybody waiting, don't you think?"

Elizabeth sighed and straightened as she agreed. Squaring her shoulders with an unconscious gesture of challenge, she crossed the room and went out the door.

It was a cloudy day, and though the double doors at the end of the hall stood open to the morning, the wide overhanging galleries on three sides of the house filled the inside with a strange twilight. As Elizabeth stepped into the hall a figure, indistinct in the dimness, jumped back.

It was a moment before her eyes adjusted, and then she saw a girl, her pale face and her gray dress with black braid trim merging into the shadows.

"Did I startle you? I didn't mean to," Elizabeth said, smiling.

"No—yes. I don't know. Are you the lady with the baby?" Nerves caused the girl to swallow convulsively, and she ducked her head so that the long brown plait hanging over her shoulder fell forward.

"Yes, I am," Elizabeth answered, an extra firmness in her voice.

"I—I heard it crying last night. Was it sick?"

"Oh, no. Just hungry, I expect."

"Are you sure? If it was sick it might die, babies do, sometimes." There was an odd note in the soft voice that made Elizabeth stare at the girl a moment.

"No, he is perfectly fine. Would you like to see him?"

A smile touched the narrow face. She took an eager

30

step forward, but as the sound of a door closing came to them her smile fled, her eyes grew large and then she turned and ran back down the hall. She entered the door on the right at the far end of the hall, and the sound of the door slamming sent echoes through the house.

A frown of puzzlement on her face, Elizabeth stared after the girl. Then, as she watched, she saw Bernard leave the room across the hall from the one that the girl had entered. He stepped up to the opposite door, knocked and went in. If he had noticed Elizabeth standing there, he gave no sign.

For breakfast there was a choice of ham, bacon, or steak, eggs fried, scrambled, poached, or boiled and fresh baked biscuits and rolls. There was also conserve, fig, pear, or peach, and fresh strawberries from the plantation garden. Elizabeth, feeling a little light-headed at such plenty, made her choice and sat down. Grand'mere was already seated. They made polite conversation about the baby, the morning, and how they had slept, but the older woman's eyes had a shuttered look and she did not mention the episode of the spiders again.

Darcourt lounged into the room, and an uneasy silence fell. He wore a bottle green frock coat with a black arm band, a black cravat which, together with a black and green patterned waistcoat, nearly hid his white shirt, and nankeen riding breeches tucked into glassily polished boots.

He gave Elizabeth a bow and a lazy grin as they were introduced, but though there was a gleam of interest in his eyes, there was such a small amount of surprise that she could only suppose that he already knew about her. He greeted her appropriately and turned to the sideboard to fill his plate. Then Bernard entered with Celestine on his arm.

Celestine, dressed in a late mourning dress of lavender silk with an amethyst pin on a black ribbon at her throat, curtsied prettily to Grand'mere, dimpled at Darcourt, and was graciousness itself to Elizabeth. But since such extreme graciousness implied a certain amount of condescension, Elizabeth's smile in return was small.

31

"You have come out of black!" Darcourt exclaimed, setting his plate on the table. "The sun may shine again!"

Celestine frowned with downcast eyes at such levity, and at such notice being paid to her change into colors. But Elizabeth saw her peek complacently at the hem of her dress in the small mirror set into the lower half of the sideboard.

"Are we pretending not to notice?" Darcourt raised his brows, obviously in high spirits. "Frankly I am more than tired of seeing nothing but crows. It seems to me the main occupation in this house is attending to death and mourning. I miss Felix as much as any, but he would not have liked this perpetual gloom, you know. I have never understood why we must all be plunged into black draperies for three years at the demise of every relative. Why, I know women who have not been out of the black for more than a year or two in all their lives!"

"Really, Darcourt. I can't think your remarks are in the best of taste. If I didn't know better I would think you had been at the spirit cabinet already," Grand'mere said.

"What you hear is relief that I am no longer the only member of this family not dressed like a specter of gloom."

"And so you have said countless times. You will not mind, I hope, if I point out to you that it still lacks a few days being a year since Felix passed away. But you cannot change convention to suit yourself, however much you may want to. Women of our station will continue to wear the willow in spite of you."

"I don't doubt it, poor things. No doubt before long the death of the family cat will be enough to plunge everything into black!"

As Darcourt touched a knuckle to his mustache there was such a gleam in his eye that it crossed Elizabeth's mind that he was baiting the old lady. Grand'mere apparently suspected it also, for she turned away and somewhat stiffly complimented Celestine on her toilette.

"If—if you don't like it, Grand'mere, I would be most happy to go and change again. I would not want to do anything to displease you," Celestine said in a low voice,

32

glancing up at the stern face of the old lady through her eyelashes.

"No, no. You must do just as you like. Felix was not a close connection, merely a fourth cousin, I believe. You have behaved with the greatest propriety in wearing black for so long," Grand'mere replied, unbending.

Celestine thanked her softly, smiling a little as she kept her eyes on her plate.

Darcourt turned to Bernard, inviting him to go riding. Bernard refused but there followed a vigorous discussion of the merits of the various saddle horses in the stable. Elizabeth listened with interest until Darcourt noticed the light in her eyes.

"Are you a rider?" he asked.

She very nearly answered in the affirmative, hoping she would be invited to ride some of the magnificent sounding horses in the stables, but she remembered in time that Ellen had not been a rider. Ellen had never liked getting dirty and overheated, even before her bout with malaria, and then she had been advised to stay out of the sun. Quickly Elizabeth shook her head, summoning a deprecating smile.

"Too bad. I had hoped for company," Darcourt said, and then forgot her. But she found Bernard watching her, a tiny frown between his eyes.

As the morning advanced the cloud cover burned away and the sun came out bright and golden. Drawn by its dazzling light and the fresh scent of spring from the new green growth, Elizabeth wandered out onto the front gallery and stood with her back against a pillar. The soaring height of the pillar and the upper gallery hanging high above her head made her feel small and insignificant. A part of her doubted that she would ever feel that she belonged to such grandeur, that it was comfortable and ordinary.

It was a fairly new house, she knew, built only three years before with a portion of the profits from several bountiful years in the cane fields. There was a smell of mortar rising from the brick floor beneath her feet and a suspicion of the scent of new lumber lingering still under the overhanging roof. The sun gleamed on the line of white pillars marching across the front of the house and cast trembling shadow patterns of the oak leaves onto the floor.

Elizabeth raised her face to the touch of the sun. It was a beautiful day, a day to be at peace with the world and yourself. The thought brought a wry smile to her mouth. She pushed away from the pillar and moved on down the gallery.

The wide colonnaded galleries that bounded the house on three sides invited strolling. They gave the house an open, airy look that detracted from its square bulk. They also shaded the inside rooms from the force of the semi-tropical sun. They remained cool and comfortable throughout the long summers, with the help of the ceilings and the thick plastered walls. The shade of the oaks, a natural grove of mixed live oaks, white, and red oaks, contributed to the aura of coolness. They stretched away on all sides, the oaks, old, huge, with blue lichen clinging to the bark of their wide spread arms. They wore the old rags of Spanish moss, hanging in tatters from them, with pride.

The light breeze moving through the trees swayed the gray moss back and forth and brought with it the heady fragrance of sun-warm sweet olive. Elizabeth stopped, looking around her for the shrub. She had discovered it growing at the corner of the house near the back wall when the sound of a voice came to her through the nearest open window.

"I am sorry, Madame, if I disturb you at your correspondence, but I must speak with you. I cannot see you alone now that the child and his nurse have been brought into your room." There was a note of reproach in the French maid's voice.

The rustle of silk, as if someone turned, could be heard, and then Grand'mere's voice came sharply. "Well, Denise?"

"My room, Madame. My eyes never closed the whole night long. It is an impossibility for me to relax. I am with that one so much. It is too much to ask that I sacrifice my nights also. You must not ask this of me!"

34

"Why not, pray?" The old lady's words were clipped, even.

"Madame knows why. It is inhuman to ask. Please have some consideration for my feelings."

"Are your feelings more to be considered than the welfare of my great-grandson? No. Give me no more whining. You have been with me a number of years, Denise, and I would not like to dispense with your services, but if you will enact to me such tragedies then I must think of dismissing you."

"Oh, no, Madame! I could not bear—"

"I will give you a character and send you back to the city in my carriage. You cannot expect more than this. I dare say you will find a new situation in a month or so."

"How can you say so, after the years I have served you? New Orleans will be full of the yellow fever in a few more weeks, and—and I am no longer familiar with the new modes from Paris. I would so much prefer to stay here." There were tears in Denise's voice, and Elizabeth found herself in sympathy with the haughty maid now being so humbled.

"Tears? All this for my sake, Denise? I think not. No, for your new position you must stipulate that you want to go to someone enroute to White Sulphur Springs or one of the other resorts for the summer to escape the fever." Grand'mere's voice went relentlessly on. "And as for being no longer *comme il faut* with fashions, I suggest you seek another old lady to bully, someone fat and dull who will not care to be so modish."

"Madame!"

"Or perhaps, since you have become so friendly with Madame Alma you might ask her to allow you to share her room."

"I have done so, but Madame Alma refused."

At the maid's whispered reply the old lady gave a bark of laughter.

Elizabeth was uncomfortably aware that she was eavesdropping, but she hesitated to move away for fear she would attract their attention or make some sound on the rough brick floor. It had sounded as if the maid was frightened to stay in the back bedroom, but why? Whom had she spoken of as *that one*? Elizabeth could not help but feel sorry for the maid, despite the fact that the woman had been less than pleasant to her. There was such a chilling implacability in the old lady's voice, such ruthlessness in her handling of the situation. Elizabeth was not at all surprised when the Frenchwoman suddenly capitulated and agreed in a subdued murmur to speak no more of the matter.

"Denise!"

The woman's answer came from farther away as though she had started to leave the room. "Yes, Madame?"

"The spiders, you know of them?"

"A thing like that does not remain a secret in a household where the linens are washed by servants."

"Of course. I have no idea where the blame lies, but I was distressed, most distressed, by the incident. All our lives were endangered, that of my grandson, even my own, in a most stupid and reckless manner. I will be displeased if there is a recurrence of anything of a similar nature.

"I assure Madame that I had nothing to do with it. I swear!"

"It doesn't matter. You will remember what I have said. Whoever the culprit may be, I deem it your duty to prevent such a thing from happening again."

"Madame, I beg of you, be reasonable—"

"That will be all."

"Please, Madame—"

"I said that will be all."

Elizabeth heard the door of the room closing, and quiet descended. Overhearing the autocratic manner in which Grand'mere spoke to her personal servant, hearing the cold voice, had brought home something that she had begun to forget while in the old lady's presence. Despite the consideration, despite the smile and the concern for her comfort, Grand'mere had no use for her personally. She was as indifferent to Elizabeth's ideas and to her supposed rights as Joseph's mother as she was to Denise's pleas and protests. Grand'mere would remain pleasant, even considerate, as long as Elizabeth's wishes did not clash with her own.

Carefully she turned and began to retrace her steps back along the gallery. Then she saw Bernard.

He stood with his arms folded, leaning against one of the columns. His face was a mask of immobility, but its very blankness was proof that he had seen her listening to his grandmother's conversation. Why hadn't she coughed or made some noise to let them know she was there? Too late she realized that she had not wanted them to know. In her need to know more about the family, she had allowed her curiosity to overcome her scruples. But though she felt the heat of a blush rising to her cheeks, she had no intention of standing there like a cat caught with cream on its whiskers. Summoning a cool smile she continued walking and would have passed him if Bernard had not put out his hand.

"Could you spare me a few minutes of your time, Madame? There is some business of your husband's estate that must be settled."

"Yes, of course," she replied.

"In the library then, if you please."

She inclined her head and walked on beside him as he straightened and strolled toward the front of the house.

"You have a beautiful home," Elizabeth said, for something to break the silence.

A sardonic smile touched his mouth and was gone. "You think you can be happy here, then?"

Elizabeth admired the house but she was not awed by it like a gawking country girl, and she resented the implication that she must be. Still, she answered mildly. "It's early to tell, but I am sure I shall be."

"Are you?"

Something in his voice brought back the creeping horror of the spiders spreading out over the sheet of her bed, and she did not answer. She went ahead of him through the front door, which he held open for her.

The butler stationed in the wide central hall jumped to open the library door, his black house slippers making no sound on the marble tiles. They passed through the door and it was closed behind them. Bernard drew forward a chair for her, and then seated himself behind the desk.

As he sorted the papers on his desk and took a bundle

of documents tied with blue ribbon from a drawer, Elizabeth watched him covertly. After the excitement of the night before, she had forgotten Grand'mere's hint that Bernard had something he wished to discuss with her. She had no idea what it could be and she could feel her nerves tightening. What could the business of Felix's estate have to do with her? Her father had never confided the business details of their property to her mother or to Ellen or herself, and she had had no reason to suppose that things would be different in her pose as Felix's widow. The legalities were the province of men. She knew absolutely nothing of Felix's affairs. She was on shaky ground. The only thing that gave her the confidence to sit quietly and wait for Bernard to begin was the reflection that Ellen was unlikely to have known anything of them either.

His papers in order, Bernard leaned back in his chair, one hand rubbing at his chin.

"It's odd," he said pensively. "You are not at all as I pictured you."

Apprehension ran along her nerves, and then subsided.

"No?"

"From Felix's letters I pictured a sweet, fragile creature. One now bowed down with grief, of course."

Letters? Elizabeth hardly noticed the soft sarcasm. She swallowed hard and hoped that he would attribute her sudden lack of color to pain.

"Not everyone puts their grief on display, Mr. Delacroix."

"No." He glanced down as he uttered the emotionless monosyllable, and then looked up again. "You have not, I think, always been well?"

Careful. A warning whispered in her mind, but she did not heed it.

"I was fully strong enough to bear Felix's son and to care for him."

"And yet he has a wet nurse?"

Color rushed in a warm wave to her forehead. This was not a subject a lady discussed with a man. Her hands were in her lap and she kept her eyes on them, hoping he would see his error. But the silence grew long and he did not speak.

At last she said with difficulty, "Perhaps I have not been as strong as I might. Our circumstances the last few months—there was so little. We were very grateful for the draft you sent as well as your kind invitation to Oak Shade."

"Thank my grandmother. Both issued from her. You say we, I believe your sister was living with you."

"Yes. She—she is dead." The lies came harder than she had imagined, and yet it was no lie. Her sister, Ellen, was dead.

"So I understand. It must have been most distressing. A virulent fever, I think it was?"

"Yes." That was what she had written to Grand'mere when she had sent the letter saying they were ready to travel. There had been no difficulty about the handwriting. Because Ellen had been so weak, the one other letter they had exchanged had been penned by Elizabeth. A fever had seemed a reasonable ailment with which to account for her own death. There were so many fevers, most of them deadly.

He was silent. Raising her head, Elizabeth looked toward the window where dust motes drifting to the floor turned lazily in the sunshine. A bird called, the repeated two note shout of a cardinal, in the top of one of the oak trees. She could sense Bernard's scrutiny as he leaned forward and picked up a miniature sword letter opener. The action restored a portion of her composure. He was not as controlled as he would like to appear.

"Ellen Marie—" His voice was soft, but something in his tone made her turn to him quickly.

He sighed as if dissatisfied, and the suspicion flickered in her mind that he had been testing her reaction to that name. Then she dismissed the thought as a figment of her imagination. She had done nothing that she knew of to arouse his suspicion. The thought of the letters Felix might have written to his brother and his grandmother flitted across her mind. But the thought was banished when Bernard straightened in his chair as if about to speak. As she regarded him across the expanse of the heavy desk, Elizabeth thought she saw reservation lingering in his eyes. He waited a moment longer and then his dark brows lifted and he shrugged, a gesture that made him seem suddenly foreign.

"Ellen Marie—forgive me if you dislike the use of your given name, but there is already a surfeit of Madames Delacroix in this house. What I must speak to you about may be distressing to you, but it is necessary. Before my brother left Oak Shade he made his will, one of the practical but still rather grandiose gestures young men going to war are apt to make. His marriage and the birth of his son nullify this will, of course, under our laws, and your son is now heir to my brother's portion of this estate. Felix was no fool. He sent his instructions to me, and to our commission merchant in New Orleans. In the event of issue from his marriage I was to be appointed guardian to the child and director of his estate until the child reached the age of twenty-five. In addition, a small piece of property belonging to him situated on Bayou St. John was to be sold and the proceeds of the sale deposited with our commission merchant in your name. This money was to be yours to use for whatever you desired, a dress allowance if you wish. It was to give you a certain independence. It seems that Felix wanted you to feel secure. This has been done. The purchase price of twenty thousand dollars, less commission, has been deposited. You may draw on this account up to one thousand dollars at any one given time. Any sum over this amount will be subject to my approval."

Twenty thousand dollars. A wave of bitterness like pain swept over Elizabeth. She could not disguise her cold anger.

"Do you mean this money has been on deposit since Felix was killed?"

"Not that long, no. The legalities had to be observed, the sale took time to arrange and complete, and then more time for the money to change hands."

"How long?"

"Since November of last year."

"Six long months—why wasn't I informed?"

Her voice was harsh as Elizabeth realized what the money might have meant to her sister: adequate food,

40

comfort, decent medical care, a chance that she might have lived. More than that, the knowledge that Felix had loved her enough to see to her security before his death would have comforted her in her desperate grief for her young husband.

If her distress, her regret, communicated itself to Bernard he did not show it. His voice was level, with a touch of scorn, as he answered her questions.

"An invitation was extended to you to come here where you could be told as soon as the sale was completed. Believe me, we did not know of your situation until you informed us. No doubt you believe we should have made inquiries earlier into your welfare? You are right, we should have, but perhaps you will try to understand our position?

"My brother Felix was officially betrothed to Celestine before he left for Texas. He bestowed on her the family betrothal ring and they were feted with the usual parties. It was an alliance of long standing between the two families, but Celestine was very young and disinclined to be left, a bride, so soon after the wedding, and so it was postponed until Felix returned from the fracas. He considered this jaunt to war in no more serious a light than a protracted hunting trip. We all did."

Bernard's face looked drawn, and Elizabeth realized again as his hand clenched on the letter opener that his control was on a tight rein.

"Imagine our surprise," he went on, turning the tiny sword in its scabbard over in his hands, "and yes, our dismay, when Felix wrote to tell us that he had met another woman and that he intended to marry her. By the time his letter reached us the deed was done. Naturally we waited to hear more. And then he was killed in battle. We were stunned. Again we waited. It seemed so unlikely. Impossible. I can't think how to make you understand. You have no idea of how uneventful, how circumscribed by tradition and convention our lives are. We received Felix's instructions written before the tragedy at Goliad and the machinery was set in motion to carry them out, but we felt we should move with caution. I considered going myself to Texas to see you, to investigate——"

41

"In short to see what kind of woman your brother had married. Or did you think I had tricked him into marriage against his will?"

"The idea had occurred to me."

"What made you decide not to come?"

"I was needed here. We decided to wait and communicate with you by mail. In addition we had not given up hope that Felix was still alive. Often there are mistakes made on the battlefields of distant wars fought in strange countries. We waited, I suppose, for a miracle to clear all difficulties."

He confessed his faults so dispassionately that it was hard to remain angry. Elizabeth could understand his reasons for avoiding a confrontation with the woman his brother had so unexpectedly married; she could even appreciate his frankness in speaking of them. But she could not quite forgive him or conquer her resentment. She got to her feet, but he detained her with a lifted hand.

"There is one thing more. I will see to it that you receive your widow's portion as quickly as possible, however our commission merchant and the attorneys who will attend to it will need proof of your identity. I assume you have something to prove you are who you say?"

"Certainly," Elizabeth replied, trying not to let the intentness of his dark eyes half-hidden behind thick lashes annoy her further. "There is the marriage record, a copy of it, and also the Brewster family Bible. I will bring them."

"That won't be necessary."

"I insist." Elizabeth started toward the door.

"Wait. Since you are determined, we will send a servant. Your woman knows where to put her hand on the things you want?"

"Yes."

Bernard summoned the butler and gave him his instructions. Elizabeth returned to her chair, and in a moment they heard the butler calling for a houseboy to carry the message upstairs. While they waited for the request to filter through the hierarchy of the house servants, Bernard removed the necessity of making conversation by opening the mail that lay on his desk. It had arrived that morning

42

on the river packet, and it had been sent out to the house by special carrier.

The sight of the letters reminded Elizabeth of the day the invitation to Oak Shade had arrived in the hand of a passing stranger. Ellen had been in bed. Excitement had brought back some of the color to the thin face above her swollen body. They had held a conference and decided to send to the Spanish Mission for a copy of the marriage record. It had seemed at the time only a natural precaution. That it should rankle to be asked to present it now was, Elizabeth recognized, a bit of perversity.

It had been nearly two weeks before someone, a distant neighbor this time, came by to carry the message to the mission. He carried also the letter to the Delacroix from Ellen accepting their kind invitation on behalf of herself and her unborn child. She planned to go to them as soon as she recovered from her confinement. Ellen had not been proud, or rather she had been more certain of the generosity of the Delacroix than Elizabeth. The letter had also contained a vivid description of the destitution and lack of funds for the journey, a description Elizabeth found hard to put on paper even after Ellen had told her exactly what she wanted to say. Ellen had wanted to ask that her husband's people include Elizabeth in the invitation, but she would not allow it. She had wanted to be independent, to make her own way in the world, rather than to be a poor relation by marriage at the mansion called Oak Shade.

Eventually the requested record, written in pure Castillian Spanish, scrolled and dangling with ribbons and seals, had arrived. The young priest who had brought it had smiled at the maternal picture Elizabeth had made standing with the baby in her arms in the doorway of their homestead. It was a natural mistake. Before he left them he baptised the baby and led them in a rosary for the girl in the grave near the house. The name he carried back with him for the death record was Elizabeth's own. Ellen would have understood, Elizabeth was sure. Her last wish had been for Elizabeth to carry her child to her husband's family and see that he received his proper heritage.

The minutes passed and there was no sign of the

records, nor a message from Callie. Elizabeth had not had time to grow really worried, however, when Bernard, frowning at a letter in his hand, got to his feet.

"Forgive me, but I must leave you for a moment to speak to my overseer. A matter of business." Without waiting for her acquiescence he crossed the room in a few strides and was gone, the letter fluttering in his hand.

She sat alone, listening to the seconds ticking slowly by on the ormolu clock on the mantel, staring at her reflection in the crepe-draped mirror beside it. With the palm of her hand, she smoothed the arm of her chair, growing increasingly nervous and perplexed. Bernard did not return, nor did the things she had sent for arrive. At last she heard quick footsteps approaching, and she got to her feet and turned toward the door.

There was a light knock, and without waiting for an invitation Celestine swept into the room.

"I thought Bernard was here," she exclaimed, staring at Elizabeth with a wide, inquisitive glance, her full skirts swaying as she stopped.

"He was. He stepped out for a minute."

"How odd, and most inhospitable of him."

That was precisely what Elizabeth had been thinking, but she did not say so.

"I wonder what he is about. No telling. He is a very busy man. I'm sure he did not mean to desert you." Celestine's voice was smooth, but Elizabeth heard the malice, as she was sure she was supposed to.

"I expect you are right," she answered quietly.

A shadow of annoyance touched Celestine's small features. "I don't imagine it is necessary to wait. Bernard will not expect it if he has been delayed."

That seemed likely. "I was thinking of returning to my room," Elizabeth said.

"Just what I would do," Celestine agreed. "I will tell Bernard that he has been most rude and he must not treat you so. It will be a lesson to him."

That was not at all what she had intended. "Oh, no. Tell him, please, that I have gone to see about the documents he wanted."

"Oh, I was not going to wait for him now," Celestine

44

objected, her voice expressing an obvious reluctance to serve as Elizabeth's messenger. She drew back to allow Elizabeth to go through the door ahead of her.

Why then had Celestine come to the library if she did not want particularly to see Bernard, Elizabeth wondered as she went through the door and down the hall toward the stairs. The only reason she could think of was curiosity, pure feminine curiosity about what was keeping Elizabeth in the library so long.

She had put her foot on the bottom stair when a sound near the top made her glance up. She stopped, frozen into immobility, afraid to make the slightest sound.

At the top of the stairs, his blanket trailing over the edge of the top step as he kicked and waved his arms, lay Joseph.

CHAPTER 3

Footsteps echoed in the hall. Elizabeth hardly heard them.

"My apologies," Bernard began as he came in sight from the back of the long hall, then he stopped as he saw Elizabeth's rigid stance.

"Bernard, *mon cher*," Celestine greeted him, ignoring the other girl as she moved toward him with her arms outstretched. "I was looking for you."

At the top of the stairs the sound of their voices had attracted Joseph. Turning his head he saw Elizabeth and with a wide grin began to squirm, trying to turn over.

"Don't!" she cried, and picking up her skirts started up the stairs at a run. She hoped the harsh sound of her voice would hold his attention long enough for her to get to him.

Hampered by the fullness of petticoats and dress she tripped, going down to one knee, catching at the bannister. She saw the baby turning and knew even as she jerked the skirt from under her feet and started on again that she could not hope to reach him before he rolled down the stairs.

Suddenly she was pushed aside as Bernard raced up the steps two at a time. But even he was not quite fast enough. With a muffled thud followed by the rasping, throat-tearing cries of a small baby Joseph fell face down onto the next stair step.

Bernard stopped his fall as he hung half off the step. By the time Elizabeth reached his side Bernard had the baby against his shoulder.

"Give him to me," she said when they had gained the landing in the upper hallway.

Blood stained the baby's lower lip where it was already beginning to swell, but otherwise he seemed unhurt. He soon stopped crying as Elizabeth rocked him against her pounding heart, murmuring to him softly. But as her anxiety eased, anger and suspicion took its place.

"Who did this? Who in the world would do such a thing? And why?"

"I imagine your nursemaid put him down on a pallet and he got there himself," Celestine said as she leisurely climbed the stairs.

"Don't be ridiculous!" Elizabeth snapped. "Four-month-old babies don't crawl."

Celestine shrugged. "Where is his nurse then? It seems very careless to me. Perhaps you should bring in another woman for your nephew, Bernard. Someone dependable."

Bernard did not answer. Nor did Elizabeth, though Celestine's question was a good one. Where was Callie?

Turning sharply she marched across the hall with the baby in her arms. She skirted the stairwell and stepped to the door of Grand'mere's room. She pushed open the door that hung ajar but there was no one inside.

"Callie?" she called.

There was no answer. The only sound that trespassed on the silence of the room was the buzzing of a fly trapped behind the lace curtains over the window.

"Callie?"

Where could she have gone? The blankets in the cradle at the foot of the old lady's bed spilled over the high wooden side, dragging onto the floor. The sticky porridge dish from Joseph's breakfast still sat on a small table, and damp, wadded cloths from the baby's bath were piled on the floor beside a pan of water already forming a cold soap scum. Elizabeth had the feeling that some time had passed since anyone had used these things, though they had not been there when she passed through the room before breakfast.

Bernard stepped into the room behind Elizabeth. Celestine trailed after him, though her face wore a look of ill-concealed impatience. For some reason their presence was an annoyance to Elizabeth, and she moved farther into the room away from them.

Her action brought her in line with the open door of her own room. She glanced in, and then stopped, her eyes wide. From where she stood she could see Callie's feet, in her brown lisle stockings and black slippers, sprawled out on the floor with her long dress twisted around her.

"Callie—" she whispered, and the next moment she was kneeling beside her.

Callie lay on her back near the bed with one of Elizabeth's nightgowns clutched in her hand. Her face was gray and drawn, a harsh contrast to the bright madras *tignon*, or kerchief, she wore tied about her head. With the baby in the crook of her arm, there was little Elizabeth could do to help the Negro nurse. She was glad when she found Bernard beside her slipping an arm under Callie's shoulders to raise her head. As he moved her the tignon slid backward onto the floor and Elizabeth cried out as she saw that the back of it was wet with blood. There was a grim look on Bernard's face as his eyes met hers, and then his eyelids masked his expression as he curtly told Celestine to send for brandy and a *vinaigrette*.

Celestine left the room but she returned shortly.

"There was no one to send," she said, shrugging her slim shoulders.

"Where the devil are they?" Bernard rasped.

"Don't growl at me. I'm sure I don't know. I suppose

47

the yard man has commandeered the errand boys again. He was complaining yesterday because the chickens were scratching around his precious roses again. And the maids must be finished upstairs."

"Then will you at least get the brandy? The decanter is on the sideboard in the dining room. There is a silver tag on it."

"I? Wait on a servant? Are you mad, Bernard?"

"Then find Denise, find Grand'mere, but do something."

At the whiplash in his voice Celestine moved, but there was resentfulness in the look she cast at Elizabeth before she turned and went unhurriedly from the room.

By the time she returned with Grand'mere and Denise, bearing a small glass of spirit on a silver tray, Callie's eyes had fluttered open. Elizabeth put down the washcloth that she had been using to bathe Callie's face, and spoke to her softly.

Callie smiled, a vague look in her eyes, and took a small sip from the glass held to her lips. Then she tried to struggle to a sitting position.

"I shouldn't ought to be laying here. I'm all right," she said, but it was patently untrue.

Grand'mere, blaming herself for not being in her room, lamenting that she had been closeted in the sitting room, sent the French maid bustling to find bandages. Then she insisted on taking the baby while Elizabeth dressed the cut on the back of Callie's head.

"Can you tell us what happened, Callie?" she asked as she worked.

The nurse seemed groggy, her eyes were still dazed, and it seemed that she would be unable to reply. Then she took a deep breath as if gathering her strength and began in a slow, halting mutter, rambling a little as if she was not quite herself.

"Little Joseph was asleep—and I had some time—time on my hands. Didn't know what I should do—whether it was my place to straighten the bedroom what belonged to the Ol' Mis'. None of the maids—upstairs maids—would

48

come in here to clean up after breakfast. Guess nobody told them to 'tend to us. Knew how to do for you, though. I thought I would just unpack—and hang all your things in that there big wardrobe in your bedroom. That's what I was doing when you—sent after them papers. I thought we put all the papers and books and such in the bottom of your trunk—and we did too. I was just lifting that big Good Book out when I heard something funny-like behind me. 'Fore I could turn around something hit me. It hurt. That's all I knowed until I—woke up just now."

"You heard something funny. What do you mean by funny?" Bernard asked.

"Well—kinda like a laugh, only quiet. At least, I think that's what it was—"

"You didn't hear anything, see anything, else?"

"No, sir. Not that I can think of."

"The woman probably fell," Celestine said. "We can only be thankful she didn't kill the baby when she hit the floor. I wouldn't be surprised to discover that she has fits or spells of some kind."

Elizabeth was speechless with indignation, an indignation that grew as she saw Grand'mere's frown and tiny nod of agreement.

"No!" she got out at last. "You can't be serious!"

"Indeed? And why not?" Celestine demanded.

"Because—because it's impossible, that's why. You don't know anything about Callie and Joseph or you would understand."

"Oh? How interesting—" Celestine began, but Elizabeth paid her no heed.

"There now, don't listen to her, and don't tease yourself," she said to Callie as tears of pain rose in the woman's eyes.

"What she mean, about killing little Joseph? He was asleep in his bed, like I told you. That's the truth."

"I know. It happened just as you said. I believe you. We have to get you to bed now, I think. This thing can be straightened out later."

"Oh, Mis'—Ellen, those things you wanted. They in the

trunk on the bed, I expect. I must have dropped them back inside when I fell. I'm awful sorry I couldn't get them to you."

"Yes, all right, Callie. Don't worry about it. I'll find everything."

As she spoke she was urging Callie to her feet with Bernard's help. She glanced at the bed, but there was no sign of the documents she sought. She would have gone on by, leading Callie toward the trundle bed set up in the large bedroom, but Callie stopped.

"They were right there. I know they was," she said. "I had the big Good Book in my hands and that fancy paper was on top all rolled up in its leather case." She reached out and tipped the small hidebound trunk with its rounded lid toward her.

"Why, Mis'—Ellen, did you get them there things out already? They was right here, but they gone now. They gone!"

"They were here," Elizabeth said in confusion, "in this trunk." She could not imagine who would have stolen them. They were of no possible use to anyone but her. Who would have taken the risk of creeping into the room, striking Callie and as a last vicious gesture, leaving Joseph, a defenseless baby who could not possibly harm them, at the head of that long flight of stairs? Who would do all those things for something so worthless? She could not make even a guess, but the papers were gone and it was obvious that someone had taken them. Obvious to her but not to the others, she discovered when she voiced the thought aloud.

"I don't understand what you are talking about," Celestine said with slow insolence. "It seems extremely unlikely that anyone in this house would steal from *you*."

"They were there," Elizabeth repeated, her voice rising, "and now they are gone. Someone must have taken them!"

"Are you quite certain? I mean, you may have left whatever it is you have lost behind," Grand'mere suggested.

"I did not leave them behind," Elizabeth said with a measured distinctness as she regained her temper. "They have been stolen, I promise you." Though she spoke to Grand'mere she looked at Bernard.

"You believe me, don't you?"

"Well, really!" Celestine exclaimed.

"Oh yes, I believe you," Bernard said. But did he? Or was he simply smoothing over what had become an awkward moment? There was nothing in his hard black eyes to tell her.

"What is going on here? How can a person sleep with such a disturbance?"

The woman who had been introduced as Bernard's step-mother followed her harsh voice into the room. Her face was puffy with sleep and around her she clutched a yellow silk wrapper. She balanced her plump figure on the ridiculously slender heels of her yellow embroidered red satin slippers. In the bright morning light there was a blowzy overripeness about her face, and the faint suggestion of a dark mustache on her upper lip. Her blackish brown hair was slipping from the confines of a pink net snood.

When they turned to look at her she pulled the wrapper closer around her. "I could hear your voices as plain as day through the walls of my room next door. I was startled wide awake, my repose quite shattered, and I hardly slept at all last night. I'm sure every joint in my body ached, and my poor head! I am certain I have a migraine coming on. It seems little enough to ask for a bit of quiet in the mornings. It is the only time I really sleep. You all know it is, I have told you often enough."

"So you have, Alma," Grand'mere said, a dry note in her voice. "You must not let us keep you, however. We have had the merest accident here. Perhaps if Denise came to you and massaged your temples with cologne you could be easy."

"Oh yes, you are good to loan her to me. Her ministrations are helpful beyond anything I have tried. Perhaps she might be persuaded to put my hair up for me, too. Such a tedious chore and quite beyond my girl, or so it seems. She is so very clumsy, I am always surprised to find that she has not buttoned me up wrong."

"Yes, to be sure. Denise is a treasure and I am certain

she will do all that is necessary for your comfort," Grand'mere said impatiently.

"Indeed yes, Madame Delacroix," Denise said, moving with an affected stateliness to the door and holding it wide for the other woman. Alma tripped through the door and down the hall, her wooden heels clacking loudly on the polished wood of the floor.

The old lady gave a crack of laughter as she stared after her daughter-in-law, but she did not explain what had amused her, nor did her amusement last.

"Your father should never have married again," she said to Bernard in a toneless voice.

Bernard glanced toward Elizabeth, as if to remind his grandmother of her presence, but made no comment. When Elizabeth and the old lady began to make Callie comfortable on the trundle bed, he went away.

Joseph, comforted by the closeness of his nurse, went to sleep in the curve of Callie's arm. When Callie's eyes began to droop also, Elizabeth got up from the chair where she had been watching them to see that they were both going to be none the worse for their ordeal. Grand'mere had sent for her correspondence from the downstairs sitting room. As Elizabeth opened the bedroom door, Grand'mere looked up from the small portable desk she held in her lap.

"Tired?" she asked in a carrying whisper, then answered herself. "You must be. Nothing is so tiring as a fright. Come, sit here beside me and tell all about these missing items. I am not at all sure I understand."

Elizabeth complied willingly enough. When she had finished, Grand'mere sat staring at the long slender wooden pen in her hand with its sharp nib.

"You are certain, quite certain, that you brought these things with you?"

"Oh, yes, Madame. I have seen them at least twice a day since I left Texas, every time I opened the trunk. There was not that much in the trunk, after all."

"I see. And you could not have left them at some stop? Your servant could not have carelessly laid them out and forgotten to put them back?"

"I'm sure she didn't."

"It isn't impossible, you know, that she is somehow at fault and is trying to cover her guilt?"

"Not Callie," Elizabeth said firmly.

"Very well, let us look at it from our angle. Who do you think would take your papers and for what reason? You do not answer. You see?" She spread her hands.

Did the old lady really intend to dismiss what had happened so easily? Was there to be no inquiry? No alarm?

"It is like the spiders," Elizabeth suggested softly. "I do not know who did that either."

Grand'mere's face froze. "You need not concern yourself unduly, I think. There will be a complete investigation made into these matters. Bernard will see to that."

And with that Elizabeth had to be satisfied. "Excuse me," she said, and rising, left the room.

As she closed the door behind her she looked up to see Darcourt standing in the opening of the doors out onto the upper gallery. A thin ribbon of blue smoke curled up from the cigar he held between his fingers. He turned warily at her footstep, and then as he saw her he smiled and, flipping the cigar out and over the gallery railing, came toward her.

"I have been hearing about the disturbance. I feel I ought to apologize for our hospitality," he said, holding out his hand. He brushed his lips across the back of her fingers as she put her hand into his. Then, keeping her hand, he tucked it into the crook of his arm with an easy, natural gesture, and led her outside onto the gallery.

The sun had moved nearly directly overhead and the gallery was shadowed and cool. A breeze wafted across the open space, lifting the fine hair that had escaped from her tidy chignon and blowing her skirts against Darcourt's boots. Sword ferns, cascading over the sides of their wrought iron containers, made a fresh green bower around several chairs at one end of the gallery, and they strolled toward it.

As they seated themselves, Darcourt lounged back in the delicate wrought iron chair and Elizabeth found herself smiling at him with sudden friendliness. With his undemanding acceptance of her, and his admiring glances and air of relaxation, he seemed more approachable than anyone else in the house. She realized that he was exerting himself to be charming and she appreciated it. No one else had bothered.

They spoke casually about the mild spring weather, the conflict in Texas, and the likelihood of the territory becoming a state. Darcourt had no firm opinion about the latter, and little concern. In that, he reminded Elizabeth of Felix, who had marched off to war for the ideal that anyone who wanted their own government badly enough to fight for it deserved a helping hand, especially if they were Americans. Felix had gone to war for the glory and romance of battle, and for the excitement of it. She had thought for months that he had gone without a thought for his bride and the possibility of a child from his marriage with Ellen. It took some adjustment in her thinking for her to credit him with the forethought to provide for his wife. What of the child, though? Joseph was heir to his father's estate. She had been hasty in closing the discussion of money without asking Bernard about that when she had the chance. It was not enough for him to say simply that he was the baby's guardian.

"You look sad," Darcourt told her. He let the front legs of the chair he was leaning back in fall forward with a thump. "You don't have to be sad for Felix. He wouldn't want that, you know. Felix was a grand person. He never lectured or came on his high horse. He was always willing to share what he had, whether it was a drink, his mount, or his last two-bit piece. He didn't like black dresses or crepe and all that rigamarole that goes with funerals anymore than I do. He hated that mausoleum down there in the family cemetery. I'm glad he isn't in it; I'm glad they buried him where he fell."

Elizabeth looked away out over the front lawn at the new grass spreading green beneath the trees. "Since he had to die, then, yes, so am I," she answered.

"He wouldn't have wanted you to pine. He was partial to a bit of gaiety himself."

"You knew him well, it seems."

"We were like brothers, rather than half-brothers. He was closer to me than to Bernard. We liked, and disliked,

54

the same things. I know he would not have wanted you to go around looking like a—a—"

"Crow?" she supplied.

"I did call you that this morning, didn't I? I apologize, but that doesn't make it any less apt."

"Three years is not too long to mourn a loved one."

"It will be the rest of your life, if you don't remarry. You realize that will be expected of you, don't you? But three years or life, what's the difference? We will all be dead of boredom before it's over. It must be worse for a woman. A man can get away for a time, but you have to stay mewed up here like a goose in a pen."

"Please!" she said laughing. "Geese in pens are being fattened for the kill! But you were not so closely related. You shouldn't have to give up all invitations. A few quiet dinner parties can not be considered making merry, surely?"

"You don't know Grand'mere and her ideas on the strength of family ties, even those of marriage. But it doesn't matter, there aren't that many invitations to be refused."

"Aren't there neighbors, friends?"

"Oh, yes, neighbors. But few real friends. This area is filling up with Americans."

"Really now. You are as American as I am."

"In name only," he said, laughing a little. "Most of our friends and relatives live in New Orleans. We move to town during the season, that is, we have in other years. We didn't this year because we were in mourning. What was the point? The soirées, the balls, everything but the dullest of family dinner parties, would have been denied to us. I slipped into town for New Year's, drank my share of eggnog at each visit—no gentleman caller is allowed to escape until he has sampled the recipe of the lady of the house, you know."

"Yes, the gentlemen used to call upon the ladies on New Year's day when we lived in Mississippi."

"Did the young ladies expect a cornet of French confection?"

"I don't think so, but then, I was hardly out of the nursery when we migrated. What is a cornet?"

"A rolled tube of gold or silver paper, like a cornucopia, with lace frills and usually a miniature of some simpering damsel in gaudy colors."

"I see, and you gave these to all the girls—or to only one?" she said teasingly.

"Oh, I must have scattered hundreds, the ladies collect them like scalps, to prove how pursued they are. If they don't receive what they consider their due, some ladies have been known to buy a few more to supplement their collection."

"You aren't serious?"

"My word of honor." He grinned. "But of course you would never stoop to such a deceit."

"No? All is fair, they say, in love and war."

"People have been using that saying for two thousand years to excuse their misdeeds."

"Are you so virtuous, then?" she asked mildly.

"I refuse to admit to that! But I have no use for hypocrites either."

There seemed nothing to say to that. Elizabeth thought there was some meaning behind the words, but she did not feel she had known Darcourt long enough to ask him to explain.

"You enjoy the New Orleans social round?" she said after a while.

"Immensely, as long as I have the feathers to fly with."

"You prefer it to Oak Shade?" Because it was so warm and pleasant on the gallery, with the breeze sweeping now and then from around the corners of the side galleries, there was a shade of censure in the question.

"Oak Shade doesn't belong to me," Darcourt said deliberately, and then shrugged. "If it did, I don't know. I would certainly have the money to enjoy New Orleans society—besides being even more socially acceptable to all the match-making *mamans*."

"An estate is a great responsibility. You wouldn't be able to spend all your time socializing or you would be bankrupt before you knew it."

His blue eyes flashed and his teeth gleamed white beneath his dark gold mustache, as he grinned at her serious expression. "What I need, I suppose, is a position where I would be paid for making merry, say as a courtier. I would have been a huge success at the French Court a hundred years ago."

"I expect you would have," Elizabeth agreed, returning the smile, her gaze on the indention in his cheek that was almost, but not quite, a dimple. He had the ready wit, the friendliness, and the audacity that would have made a good courtier. "But being a courtier wasn't all dancing and gaiety. What about the bowing and scraping, the boot-licking and back-biting?"

"What, in a word, of the hypocrisy?"

"Yes, I suppose that is what I meant," Elizabeth admitted.

"My scruples would be as firm as rock, I expect, until they were tried." He laughed across at her, and then his smile faded. "Isn't that the way of it?"

The bitterness in his voice found an echo in Elizabeth's mind. She did not reply. The question came too close to home.

As she stared out through the tree limbs with unfocused eyes, Bernard came into view beneath them with Celestine beside him. His head was bent to her vivid upturned face as she clung to his arm with both hands. They were following the curving path of the drive, strolling apparently without destination.

"Celestine is at it again, turning Bernard up sweet. She is a heartless jade, but pretty, you must admit. She will be marrying him if he doesn't look to himself."

"Will she?" Elizabeth could not have said why the idea was so unacceptable. She did not like Celestine, but as far as she could see they were well-suited.

"She expects it, of course. Celestine was cheated of a husband—no offense intended," he added hastily as Elizabeth glanced quickly across at him. "But Celestine has no objection to Bernard as a substitute. I would not be surprised if she wouldn't prefer it."

"That wouldn't be jealousy I hear?" Elizabeth asked lightly. The subject, and the look on Darcourt's face as he watched the graceful figure of the Creole girl, made Elizabeth vaguely uncomfortable.

"Possibly." A wry look crossed his face, and then blossomed into a short laugh. "There won't be any great hurry about it. If I know Celestine, and I think I do—she has never bothered to hide her feelings from me because I am not good, affluent husband material—she will wait to see if the Delacroix still have money when this recession talk dies down."

"Are you serious?" Elizabeth asked, turning her eyes back to the couple moving slowly down the gravel drive.

Darcourt frowned as he stared after them also. "I'm not quite sure. I wish I was."

Silence descended over them and Elizabeth was thinking of an excuse to go back into the house when there came a shout.

"Darcourt! I have done it again! I left silly Denise primping and perfuming for you and—"

The girl Elizabeth had seen earlier that morning in the hall stopped short as she saw Elizabeth. Her face lost the gleeful gaiety that had given it animation and stood with wide eyes that were strangely frightened.

"What was it you did, *chère*?" Darcourt spoke to her in a soft teasing voice. He held out his hand and she came to stand beside his chair, leaning against his shoulder.

"It wasn't anything," she murmured with her eyes on the floor.

"Theresa, have you met our new sister-in-law?"

The girl shook her head, drawing close to Darcourt until she was almost hiding behind his chair. She seemed tall for her age, nearly as tall as Elizabeth, and unaccountably shy for a girl who must be almost ready to leave the schoolroom.

"Ellen Marie, my sister Theresa." He took his sister's hand, pressing it as if to give her courage, and drawing her forward. "This lady, Theresa, was Felix's wife, the mother of the baby I am sure you have heard."

"Oh, yes!" The color crept back into Theresa's oval face. "They would not let me see him. I expect it is because—"

She glanced at Darcourt and he said, "Because you have been ill."

"Yes. You have to be careful with babies, don't you?"

58

Elizabeth agreed, a sense of disquiet touching her as she saw the avid interest that replaced the shyness in Theresa's eyes. Then, as she acknowledged the introduction and asked the polite, impersonal questions expected, memory stirred. Although it was nearly midday, Theresa still wore her dressing gown. Her feet were bare and the thick rope of her dark hair hung over her shoulder. Earlier, in the hall, the girl had been wearing a dress, not a gown and wrapper. But perhaps she had been sent back to bed because of her illness, Elizabeth told herself, and dismissed it. Or she tried. But something about Theresa troubled her. The girl that stood before her with her dressing gown to the floor barely covering her slipperless feet seemed older than the girl she had seen so briefly in the hall with her skirts halfway to her ankles. She found herself wondering what she would look like with her hair up, that metamorphosis that changed a girl into a young lady. Because her mind was full of speculation she was more than cordial to her.

"You must be sure to come and see Joseph when you are well again."

"I would like that, if Grand'mere and Denise will let me," Theresa said, looking down at her fingers, which she had twisted together.

Replying to that oddly submissive tone of voice more than to the girl's words, Elizabeth said, "It is my baby, and I will certainly let you see him."

Theresa smiled up at her, a flashing radiance that was quickly gone.

A beetle, shiny and black, was crawling along the planking before them. Even as Elizabeth noticed it, Darcourt reached casually out with his booted foot and crushed it.

"Don't! Oh, don't!" Theresa cried out, clapping her hands to her ears. "Don't kill it! That sound, I can't stand that sound!"

Surprise mixed with remorse covered Darcourt's face, but he bent down and picked up the dead beetle, throwing it over the gallery railing. Then he put his arm around his sister.

"Hush, now. I just wasn't thinking. Hush." When she began to breathe normally he laughed. "Good Lord, Theresa, a man never knows what is going to set you off next. Be quiet now, that's a good girl. It's not as if you had never seen a dead bug before, not with poison in every corner to kill the creeping things."

"You don't understand," Theresa cried, hiding her face in Darcourt's shoulder. "You won't understand."

Over her bowed head, Darcourt looked at Elizabeth and lifted one hand in a helpless gesture. Elizabeth understood his predicament but felt too much of an outsider to interfere. She was afraid Theresa would reject any comfort she might offer. Darcourt continued to speak softly to his sister. Out of consideration for their privacy, Elizabeth looked away out over the railing. She sought Bernard and Celestine and saw them moving among the trees, the lavender of Celestine's dress a spot of flashing color in the shade. They had reached a wide curve in the gravel and shell drive and had turned back toward the house.

"They are coming back," she said, hardly realizing she had spoken aloud.

"Who?" With a quick swing of mood, Theresa raised her head to follow Elizabeth's gaze, her intense distress forgotten as if it had never been.

"Celestine and your brother," Elizabeth replied, glancing curiously at the girl.

A frown came between Theresa's eyes, and then her face cleared. "Oh, you mean Bernard. He isn't my brother. Only Darcourt."

"He isn't?"

Theresa shook her head, watching the couple, oblivious of Elizabeth's puzzlement.

"She means that Bernard is related to us only by marriage," Darcourt explained for his sister. "Theresa and I are not Delacroix. Our mother married into this family after our father died. Bernard and Felix were half-grown then, children of the first wife, Amelia. They were about thirteen and fifteen at the time. I think their father, old man Gaspard Delacroix, intended to give his sons the softening influence of a mother. A pity."

Elizabeth failed to see what had amused him in that last cryptic utterance, but at least he seemed inclined to talk about the family. That was more than anyone else was willing to do.

"I think Grand'mere mentioned that her son had married twice, but she didn't say how long ago it was. Do you mean that you have been living together all this time, something like fifteen years or more, and you still don't feel like brothers and sisters?"

"It takes more than time."

"Your step-father, Gaspard, is dead?"

He nodded. "Has been for nearly three years. He broke his neck in a fall from the framework of this house while it was being built."

For no reason that she could see, a shiver ran over her and the roots of her hair prickled. She looked at Darcourt and found him watching her, and she wondered if he had expected her to be shocked or to have an attack of sensibility at his revelation. His concern, if that was what it had been, was embarrassing, and she was glad when the dinner bell rang.

Darcourt walked with Theresa back to her bedroom door, and Elizabeth, after checking on Callie and Joseph, went downstairs alone. She trailed her hand down the bannister railing abstractedly. There was a feeling growing within her, not something she could catch and hold on to, just a sense of unease. It had nothing, she thought, to do with her masquerade as Ellen. And yet she was not sure. Why the necessity for quiet concerning the spiders? Why was there not more concern, more dismay, at finding Joseph taken from his bed and left so dangerously near the stairway? Or at finding Callie unconscious, the papers gone?

It was strange, and yes, alarming. Could it be that they all knew who had done these things? She placed little faith in Grand'mere's assurance that Bernard would make inquiries. What had she meant, that he would question the servants, even Denise? The French maid had been her favorite suspect for the person who had placed the spiders in her bed, but it made no sense for the woman to take the

61

papers. What would she want with them? It had certainly meant an embarrassment for her, if that was what Denise had wanted, but petty jealousy and resentment were not motive enough for endangering a baby's life.

CHAPTER 4

Just before Elizabeth reached the foot of the stairs, Bernard and Celestine came through the front door. Celestine was flushed and laughing, and a trace of humor lingered about Bernard's mouth.

The other girl looked up and saw Elizabeth standing at the bottom of the stairs. Something like triumph flashed across her face before she asked, "Has the dinner bell rung?"

When Elizabeth told her that it had, Celestine pouted.

"See there," Bernard told her. "I told you it was near one o'clock. Next time you will believe me."

"He thinks he is clever because he can tell time by the sun," Celestine confided to Elizabeth, but from the slant of her eyes Elizabeth could see that she meant to flatter Bernard.

He laughed, but gave no sign that he recognized the compliment. "We will be in the cook's black books if we are late."

"That would be a shame, no doubt," Celestine said as he hurried her up the stairs to freshen up.

"Yes, indeed. If she decides her value as a cook is not properly appreciated, she is capable of burning every dish she cooks for a solid week just to make sure we do appreciate her when she does it right."

"She wouldn't dare."

"No? That is what is known as the tyranny of house servants."

"Isn't she afraid you will have her whipped?" Celestine dragged back on the hand pulling her inexorably up the stairs so that she could manage her dress without showing her ankles.

He laughed. "Old Ernestine used to bake gingerbread boys with currant eyes for me. She knows I wouldn't do such a thing. If I did she might not bake them for my sons. Besides, it would start a war of attrition that I could not win. The upstairs maid would forget to change my bed and dust my room, my valet would shave me with cold water—"

"If he did you would have his head!"

"And on top of that Grand'mere would have a few words to say on cruelty to helpless creatures. I shiver to think of it."

"Oh, I'm sure."

Their bantering voices faded as they reached the upper hall. To be excluded from the easy camaraderie gave Elizabeth an empty feeling. But even as she acknowledged it, she realized that as long as she had to live with her deception, as long as she had to submerge her true self, then she could never be a part of it. This was one of the penalties she must pay. It might well be, she was beginning to realize, one of the lesser penalties.

Dinner, as the midday meal was called, was the main meal of the day. It was a long repast beginning with a rich seafood soup, and passing through several game and meat courses with vegetable side dishes and wines. It was completed with pastries, a berry cobbler, and three kinds of cake, all topped off with *petit noir,* black coffee in tiny demitasse cups. It was impossible for the six people gathered around the table laid with a heavy damask cloth, crystal, and silver, to make an impression on the bounty. What became of what was left? Elizabeth wondered. Did it go back to the kitchen for the servants, the fifteen or twenty that she had seen flitting around the house? If not, there would be an appalling amount of waste.

Bernard sat at the head of the table. Elizabeth had been

63

placed on his right, rather grudgingly she felt, but she might have been mistaken. His step-mother sat on his left, Darcourt was beside Elizabeth and Celestine sulked across the table from Darcourt. Grand'mere reigned at the foot of the table.

Grand'mere and Darcourt seemed to be the only ones with an appetite. Celestine picked at her food with pretty gestures while Madame Delacroix paid more attention to her wine glass. Often her gaze rested on Elizabeth, and, though her expression was vacant, Elizabeth felt that the older woman resented her presence.

Hoping to bring a friendlier light to the small black eyes, Elizabeth said, "I met your daughter, Theresa, this morning. She is a very pretty girl. I hope she will be able to join us at the table before too long."

Alma Delacroix stared, her glass suspended halfway to her mouth. "It is most unlikely," she said finally in a repressive tone, and then swallowed her wine in a gulp.

"Oh? Is she very ill then? She didn't appear to be."

"Appearances can be extremely deceptive." She allowed her thick white eyelids to fall over her eyes, gazing down at her empty glass.

Elizabeth pressed her lips together, but she had no choice other than to accept the rebuff.

The butler moved quietly around the table, refilling the water and wine glasses, proffering dishes and murmuring a word or two of praise for a particular dish as he offered it. The clink of dishes and rattle of cutlery were loud in the unnatural quiet.

Grand'mere, acting as hostess, made no effort to introduce a topic of discussion or in any way ease the strain. At last Celestine and Darcourt began a desultory conversation about their friends in New Orleans. Though the people they were talking about were strangers, it was better than nothing.

The table had been cleared, the desserts served, and coffee poured before a comment was directed at her again.

"I believe I have found a reliable woman for Joseph," Grand'mere told her. "A little older than your woman, perhaps, and used to babies. She has had four or five of her own, I forget which, all still living. She has expressed

64

herself as happy to nurse Joseph in addition to her own child. Natural, of course. She has ambitions to serve inside the big house. She has been working in the quarter's nursery."

"What?" Elizabeth could not believe it.

"I said—"

"No, I know what you said. But are you really suggesting that I replace Callie?"

"I am. I was quite willing to have her in my room temporarily, but I really prefer to have one of our own people with me. Now that she has proven herself negligent, I have had to move more quickly than I intended. No matter—"

"But it does matter!" Elizabeth said the first thing that entered her head to stop the complacent flow of words. "Callie has not neglected Joseph. It was not her fault that she was unable to protect him."

"Surely you don't believe that? Who would strike her? It is ridiculous on the face of it. The lazy chit probably put the baby on the floor to play and then went to sleep. It would not be unnatural after the long trip and her interrupted nights."

"Joseph could not have gotten out of the room and across the hall."

"How do you know? He can turn over, can't he? And pull himself along on his elbows if he sees something he wants?"

"Yes," Elizabeth was forced to admit. "But it would take hours."

"Pish and tush."

"Do you think Callie cut her own head to make it bleed, or struck herself on the back of the head until she was unconscious? And what of my missing documents?"

"She lost them no doubt and was afraid of the consequences, so she took this way out."

"I refuse to believe it." Elizabeth's voice shook with anger that was laced with fear. She was powerless and she knew it. There was little she could do if they decided to pay no heed to her wishes. She could take Joseph and leave the plantation, but it would be a struggle to support herself in such a case, much less a tiny baby. Alone she might find a place as a governess or a seamstress or milliner apprentice, but who would give a woman with a child such a position?

"Nevertheless," Grand'mere began, but Elizabeth interrupted.

"I cannot allow Joseph's routine to be upset like that. Callie would give her life for him. They are used to one another, and I trust her completely. If you don't care to have Callie with you at night then she and Joseph can come into my room. I am not sure but what I would not prefer it, especially after the peculiar things that have happened since I arrived."

The boldness of this declaration seemed to take the old lady aback, but she recovered swiftly.

"Really, you are very young. You would do well to be advised by older and wiser heads. I have only the child's safety and comfort in mind. After all, I am his great-grandmother."

"I appreciate your concern, and I am grateful for it. But though I dislike having to remind you, I am Joseph's mother."

Without waiting for a reply Elizabeth stood, dropped her napkin on the table, and walked away. Bernard and Darcourt got to their feet as she rose and stood until she was out of the room. She carried with her the comforting memory of Darcourt's low voice, "Bravo," spoken as she passed his chair.

A kind of furious elation carried her up the stairs. Once in her room she called Callie to her and questioned her closely about what had happened. The interview did little good except to strengthen her conviction that Callie was telling the truth. By the time she had satisfied herself, her elation had ebbed away. She warned Callie of what Grand'mere intended to do, gave her strict instructions designed to protect both herself and the baby, and sent her back to Joseph.

She would have liked to hold Joseph herself. It gave her a strange sort of confidence and reassurance. But he was asleep, and after his accident on the stairs that morning she did not want to wake him. Moreover, according to Callie, there was an unwritten law that you do not wake a sleeping child.

66

She sat beside the window, looking out at the trees beyond the gallery. The woods seemed to press up to the house, giving her the suffocating feeling of being closed in. She recognized vaguely that a part of this sensation was due to a gnawing sense of being trapped in this situation of her own making. And she had not yet been in the house twenty-four hours, she reminded herself grimly.

She heard Grand'mere go into the next room and speak to Callie. They kept their voices low so as not to wake the baby. The last thing Elizabeth wanted was to renew her quarrel with Grand'mere, and yet as long as she stayed in her room she could be forced into it.

Moving quietly, Elizabeth crossed the bedroom and let herself out into the hall. The small errand boy was asleep on his bench, his hands under one cheek, and his bare feet drawn up onto the red velvet upholstery. The doors along the length of the hall were closed. Elizabeth surmised that the other members of the family were indulging in the custom of the siesta, a desirable thing after that enormous meal.

Her soft morocco slippers made little sound on the floor. They were made for wearing in the house, and she thought of going back to change them, but decided against it. The house was growing steadily more oppressive. She could not bear the thought of being forced to contain her temper while she endured another homily from Grand'mere.

Outside the sun was warm, the breeze fresh. Imperceptibly her depression began to lift as she walked. Feeling, perhaps unreasonably, that spying eyes watched her from the house, she stepped into the shadows of the trees and went deeper into their shade. She lost sight of the house, though she knew where it was located. A faint trail snaked through the high grass, and wandering aimlessly, enjoying the warmth of the sun and the clean sweet fragrance of growing things, she followed it. Her footsteps on the thick layer of leaf mold released the smell of decaying vegetation, a not unpleasant smell in the fresh air. Dog-tooth violets hid beneath the leaning stems of last year's dried weeds. Dark green vines of yellow jasmine with a few lingering yellow trumpets hung from the trees, mingling with the brown vines of wild grape. Some effort had been made to tame the profusion of growth, but it was wilder here than among the oaks on the front lawn. Actually, she thought that the word lawn was a misnomer for the stretch of tree-studded acreage that lay between the house and the dirt road.

In a small clearing she discovered a great, white-blossomed dogwood that spread its branches like an umbrella above her head. It was the largest tree of its kind that she had ever seen.

Somehow the sight of it, so strong, so sure of the rightness of its position, soothed her. The four petals of the white flowers with their brown indentations, symbols of the cross and the nail scars, were calming in their religious significance. She did not pray, and yet the peace of prayer came to her with a measure of certainty, the certainty that what she was doing was for the best. She stood looking at it for a long time, and then she turned back the way she had come. There was no escape from what she was doing. It had to be right.

She was watching the ground, holding her skirts above the snatching brambles, when she became aware of movement on the edge of the trail. A man pushed away from the tree against which he had been leaning and confronted her on the narrow track. She had the impression for a fleeting moment that he had been there some time, watching her. Her earlier feeling of being watched returned to her.

Suppressing a start, she dropped her dress over her ankles and stood with her hands clasped tight as Bernard came toward her.

"It is a nice tree, as trees go," he drawled, "but I never knew it to be quite so interesting."

When Elizabeth did not answer he went on. "How do you like our wilderness? Grand'mere wants to clear this area and underplant the larger trees with some kind of shrubs from the Orient. Personally, I like it the way it is."

"I imagine it would be lovely either way."

"A diplomatic answer. I am surprised."

There was a lift to his eyebrows that Elizabeth did not

68

particularly like. Her own tone when she answered him was cool.

"Are you?"

"You were not exactly diplomatic with Grand'mere at dinner. She only wants what is best for the baby. She is not trying to take anything from you, as you seem to imagine."

She stared at him. "Do you think Callie was to blame for what happened this morning? Do you really believe she was pretending to be unconscious?"

"I can see no other alternative but to believe it."

"Can't you? I can." Her voice was rising but she could not help it. His bland assurance was intensely irritating, as had been his attitude from the moment he stepped into the path.

"You think one of this family, in full daylight, attacked your servant, and leaving her unconscious removed your property, took the baby from his bed and left him at the head of the stairs where he could be hurt, even killed. Such a suggestion is preposterous. More than that, it is an intolerable insult!"

The fire of anger in his slitted eyes was frightening, but Elizabeth refused to be intimidated.

"And I tell you Callie loves Joseph as if he were her own. She would never allow him out of her sight, if she could help it, and even if he could have gotten himself that far. And she does not lie!"

"Just like all women, you are being emotional. Consider, Callie is a slave. Suppose she does love Joseph as her own? What if she knew your papers were gone and that she was at fault? Would she not be afraid that if her carelessness was discovered Joseph would be taken from her? That she might be sent to the fields, or even sold? What would be more natural than for her to try to place the blame elsewhere, even to hurting herself to make it convincing?"

"Callie knows I would never sell her," Elizabeth said scornfully.

"But she no longer belongs to you."

"What do you mean?"

"A woman's property becomes her husband's when she marries," he answered, grim satisfaction in his voice. "Now that Felix is dead, his property and yours belongs to his son. And," he ended softly, "I am in charge of the estate until Joseph reaches his majority."

Her first thought was that Felix would not have done such a thing. Then she thought of Ellen, so fragile, so in need of protection from the least unpleasantness, and dread crept into her mind. She recognized her own ignorance of the law, but she could see no reason for Bernard to lie. What he had said could be checked with an attorney. She remembered that earlier, when he had told her about the money Felix had arranged to be put in his wife's name, he had said that the amount would be controlled by himself. Helpless rage swept over her, and she spoke without taking time to think.

"Perhaps you can sell Callie, I don't know. But I will tell you this. If you do, or if you try to replace her, then I will take Joseph and leave here immediately!"

Not a muscle moved in his face. "You may go when you wish. But you will not take Joseph. As his legal guardian I forbid it."

His mouth was stern beneath hard black eyes. Dark in appearance, dark in spirit, Elizabeth thought. He was so different from his brother. Felix had been an example of the fiercely fun-loving type of Creole. He had been quick-tempered and reckless in anger, but his anger had always been short-lived. Bernard seemed to be the opposite type, the dark Creole. They were slow to anger or to judge, but equally slow to forgive. They made bad enemies, or good priests. Cynical by nature, they were not men who were easy to deceive.

Elizabeth did not doubt him. She believed that he did have the power to withhold Joseph from her. It seemed all a piece with the direction her life had taken in the past few years. A malevolent fate had decreed that she would be trapped at Oak Shade, in that cold temple draped in mourning with its cold, heartless inhabitants. It was the inevitable outcome of that string of deaths which included those of her father, Felix, and Ellen. It was also the result

70

of her own try at deception. There was even, she felt, a certain strange justice in it.

Something hard and heavy settled in her throat. Not trusting herself to speak, she swung around and walked away a few paces.

Finally she said over her shoulder, "Felix must have trusted you very much.

"I suppose he did."

"You will understand, I hope, if I am not quite as trusting as he? I think that you mentioned a letter this morning?"

"Perhaps you would like to see it? It was sent on to my attorney, but I can, of course, send for a copy."

It was not the answer that she wanted. She had hoped to be shown all of the letters Felix had written while Bernard searched for the particular letter containing the instructions concerning legal affairs. The thought of those letters was a canker in her brain. She could not rest until she had seen them for herself and discovered what they contained about Ellen, and about her sister, Elizabeth. Thoughtfully she stared down at her hands with her head bent.

At that evidence of what he thought to be a lady-like submission Bernard stepped toward her.

"This will be difficult for you to accept," he said, a vestige of warmth seeping into his voice, "but I am not much happier with the situation than you are. The responsibility was there and clearly I had to accept it. I don't say that it is fair for the guardianship of your son to be out of your hands, but then again it is not, strictly speaking, unfair. Joseph's inheritance, his land, his holdings, march with mine. The burden of management is not something to be undertaken lightly, certainly not by a woman. Who do you think is better qualified to guard Joseph's interests than I? His interests are the same as my own."

Though his explanation mollified her somewhat, she could not help but question him. "You mention Joseph's land, but where is it? And what of this house?" She waved in the general direction of Oak Shade, which was hidden beyond the trees.

71

"Oak Shade happens to be mine, but you need not worry about what belongs to Joseph. There were six different plantations in my father's estate, each with a habitable house upon it. Of these I hold three, including Oak Shade. Joseph now has two, since the sale of the smallest of his holdings to provide your pin money as Felix directed."

Elizabeth blinked at this casual mention of what would no doubt comprise thousands of acres of land, and at the reference to her twenty thousand dollars as "pin money."

"There are two reasons, you can see, for what you may regard as an injustice. Felix wanted to shield you from all that is disagreeable and provide someone to help you raise his son in the event that he would be unable to do so himself."

"Yes, I—I can appreciate that," Elizabeth said, but her understanding did not take away the rankling feeling of helplessness brought on by Bernard's use of his authority.

A smile lurked in his eyes. If he sensed her reservation he did not show it.

"Shall we call an end to our differences then?"

There was nothing else for her to do but agree and place her fingers in his outstretched hand.

Because she felt that she had been less than gracious in her capitulation, Elizabeth tried to keep up a conversation on the way back to the house. She could not afford to sulk. Her position had become too precarious to encourage enmity. But though her mind told her this was the intelligent course, her heart was unconvinced.

The sun went behind a bank of clouds. The wind began to rise, sending mares' tails chasing around the horizon and flattening the grass beneath the trees. It caught at her hair, loosening auburn wisps from her chignon, and pressed her skirts against her. There was a dampness in the wind's breath, a foretaste of rain. Unconsciously Elizabeth hurried her footsteps toward the house.

"Wait." Bernard put out a hand to catch her arm.

Obediently she stopped and turned to him.

The wind ruffled the dark hair that waved back from his forehead, and his eyes were narrowed against it. The collar of his black velvet frock coat with its black satin piping flapped against his shoulder.

"Come this way," he said abruptly.

They circled the house, coming up behind it. Through the trees she could see the two doublestoried, galleried back wings built at right angles to the house. In their upper stories they housed the house servants, while downstairs were the kitchen, the dairy, the still room, and the laundry. She knew that a wagon road led to the quarters of the field hands. Along the road between the quarters and the big house stood the smokehouse, the plantation jail and store, the barns and their adjacent stables and carriage house, the cooperage and the tool shed. It was a compact village of buildings hidden from the main house, its noise and confusion separated from the house by nearly two miles of woods. Somewhere beyond the slave quarters, the far stretching open fields began.

Directly behind the house a bayou looped and turned. A trail of beaten earth followed the curves of the bayou, and they walked along it, again losing sight of the house. Except for an edging of Louisiana phlox, its lavender blue flowers dancing in the wind, the path was clear, the way open. Here the undergrowth had been cleared from beneath the trees so that the ground was carpeted with leaves, but still there was an element of wildness in the intense encroaching quiet and the view of the untouched primeval forest seen on the opposite bank of the bayou. The tall, moss-hung cypress trees soared above them near the water's edge. Bamboo, the native cane, stood in clumps. Turtles slid from their logs, falling into the water with plopping sounds, as they passed. The greenish black water of the slow moving bayou reflected the overhanging trees, the high, scudding, gray clouds, and a small white pavilion.

Bernard used his handkerchief to dust a place for her on the bench that ran around three sides of the pavilion. Then he stood with his back against one of the columns that made up the walls, tucking his handkerchief back into his pocket.

"When he designed this place my father intended it as a

destination at the end of a walk, a place for the ladies to rest. No one comes here, however. I don't know why. But we are unlikely to be interrupted."

Elizabeth thought she knew why no one came. It had a cold feeling to it, like the house it resembled, except there were no walls to give the illusion of privacy. It was open, airy, nothing more than a roof, a floor, the bench, and four walls of small-scale columns. The wind swept through it, sending a dry leaf scuttling across the floor. Elizabeth glanced at the sky, judging the possibility of rain.

"I won't keep you long," Bernard said. "There is a point or two that still needs clearing up. I don't want you to feel that I am heaping all of this on you at once, but it is important.

"Yes. Go on," Elizabeth encouraged him when he paused. He seemed uncomfortable, which struck her as so unusual that she became alert.

"You probably are aware that the country is in an economic panic," he began doubtfully.

Though she had heard the expression, Elizabeth was by no means certain of exactly what it meant. Still, she knew that it had a direct bearing on money being scarce, and she was no stranger to that. She nodded.

"It affects us here with low prices for our produce. Cotton is at seven cents a pound; that is like giving it away. We grow some of the best staple in the South here on Oak Shade, and I would rather let it rot in the barns than let it go for next to nothing. I have been holding it since it was harvested, hoping for a rise in price, but so far things have gone the other way. Still, the economy cannot stay this way forever. If I can hold out long enough I stand to gain. In the meantime the money is tied up in the bales sitting in the barns and warehouses, and there are still the hands to feed, the expenses to be met, and a new crop to plant. More than that, I believe cotton will go as low as five cents per pound. Anybody with extra cash could buy up some of the cotton that is going begging, and take advantage of some of the acreage that has come onto the market now that so many planters are failing."

He stopped as though expecting a comment, but when Elizabeth made none he went grimly on.

74

"The problem is cash. We are by no means poor, but like most planters we carry little cash reserves. This new house and its furnishings ate up most of my father's cash resources. Profit the year before last was turned into more land, more hands, more equipment to work the land, and clothing, food, and medical supplies for the thousand or more slaves on the plantations. It mounts up. And as I said, we have not yet realized our profit from this past year.

"I can borrow, but I dislike doing it. The interest would have to be deducted from any profit made, payments would have to be managed—and the profit may be a year in coming, or longer, depending on how soon the economy recovers."

Catching the trend of his discourse, Elizabeth thought she knew what was coming, yet she could not be sure. It seemed so unlikely that she kept quiet, letting him complete his explanation and come to the point.

"What I have in mind is this. The money set aside for your use is idle. It is being held in trust for you. If it was put to use it could be increased by as much as a third."

"Or lost?"

"The possibility is remote. The country, and the Delacroix holdings, would have to collapse first."

"You want to use my widow's portion for these investments rather than borrowing?"

"Yes. The money is in my hands, of course, but I would prefer to have your approval. You will not lose by it, I promise you."

There was something ominous in what he had said, but she could not quite put her finger on it. "I thought I was not allowed to use more than a thousand dollars at any one time."

"You are not, not without my consent. That proviso was merely to protect you from fortune hunters and other hangers-on when you go into town, New Orleans. Naturally I stand in a somewhat different case." A smile flitted across his face.

"Naturally," Elizabeth repeated dryly, unmoved by his smile. Even as she put her questions to him she knew that she had not the slightest intention of granting his request.

Why she led him on she could not say, unless it was to raise his hopes so that his frustration and humiliation would be greater when she refused him. But refuse him she would. He would pay for his earlier high-handed treatment of her. He was not quite all-powerful. His need must be very great, she told herself in puzzlement, for him to deliver himself into her hands in such a manner. Or perhaps he had not accepted her, the young, grieving widow, dependent on him for her "pin money," to have the temerity to refuse his request.

She rose suddenly to her feet.

"I don't believe I can do what you ask," she said in a firm voice. "I could not possibly take the risk with my only means of security."

"Don't answer too hastily," he said softly. "You may, perhaps, reconsider."

There was no anger in his face and the fact worried her. "I can't think that will be necessary."

"I disagree. You see, before your portion can be made over to you, you will have to establish your identity. Until such time the money will remain in my hands."

"And at your disposal? I don't think it is likely, at least, not legally." There was a strain in Elizabeth's voice. What she had intended to be a cool sarcasm came out at a near whisper.

"You are wrong. The disposition of the money has been left entirely at my discretion. And I will do what I think best for you." His words were accompanied by a mock bow that in its civility struck Elizabeth with a greater chill that what he had said.

There was a silence. The wind made a sighing sound in the surrounding trees, and her hot cheeks.

"Why did you give yourself the trouble of asking me, then?" she asked at last.

He did not answer that. "Come, let us go back to the house."

Elizabeth looked away from his outstretched hand. "I think I would rather stay here, for a little while."

"Very well. Don't tarry long. It will be raining soon."

Turning on his boot heel, he walked away. The soft black of his coat faded quickly into the wood shadows.

76

Elizabeth stared after him. Suppose he had asked her permission to use the money in the nature of a test? Suppose he had wanted to see if she would react as the sweet, fragile girl Felix had described in his letters? Those letters. They haunted her.

Another suspicion came to her. Her lack of identification was to Bernard's advantage. He would keep the widow's portion in his control until she could produce proof that she was who she claimed. Who else had as good a reason for taking the documents that would identify her as Ellen? He had left her in the library abruptly, and he had been near the stairs when she had left the library. Was it possible that he had just put Joseph down and descended the stairs when he heard her leaving the library and had quickly stepped out of sight until he could appear from the back of the hall to make it look as if he had come from the outside?

In a dazed comprehension she let her suspicions go a step further. What would become of the money left in Bernard's care if anything should happen to her? It appeared that he would have the unhampered use of it in that case. And if something happened to Joseph also? Bernard would be a direct beneficiary as the child's next of kin!

A cold fear struck at her heart. If she was right then menace lay in wait for her in the house beneath the shade of the oaks. She was involved in a battle of nerve and wit, one from which there could be no withdrawal; one in which defeat was unthinkable. And Bernard was the enemy.

Bernard.

It occurred to her that his kind of Creole darkness was associated not only with priests, but with pirates. Those who take what they want without respect for the rules of warfare. Those who leave no survivors to bear witness.

A crackling sound in the underbrush behind the pavilion pierced her abstraction. She jumped to her feet, alarmed more by her thoughts than by the noise. It came again, nearer this time, and then it took on the measured rustle of hurried footsteps. A figure appeared, moving through the trees, looking neither left nor right. It was a woman hurrying along with a rolling crouch, a shawl drawn over her head.

Where was she going? Where had she been? As far as Elizabeth knew there was nothing in that direction from the house except miles of virgin forest. Was she going to the big house? She seemed to be.

It was only after her shambling shape had vanished from sight among the trees that recognition came to Elizabeth. It had been the woman who complained of migraines, the one who looked as though she would not dream of stirring beyond the walls of the house. It had been Darcourt's mother, Madame Alma Delacroix.

CHAPTER 5

Elizabeth lay in bed with her hands clasped behind her head, staring up into the darkness of the canopy above her. The mosquito netting enclosed her like a misty prison. Through it she could see occasional lightning flashes, dim, but growing slowly brighter. The storm had been building all the afternoon and evening. The wind sweeping in the window billowed the netting, so that it rose and fell around her. She reached for the sheet to cover her bare arms.

She was not sleepy. It had been a long time since she had heard a sound from the rooms on either side of her own, or from the rest of the house. She had come upstairs early. She had felt totally unable to sit quietly in Bernard's presence while her suspicions of him sang like a dirge in her head. She had played with Joseph a little while, but the sight of the puffy cut on his lip had driven all thought of sleep from her mind.

The night before, tiredness had been like a draught of laudanum sending her into dreamless slumber, but tonight her nerves were stretched taut. Sleep was impossible.

The sound of a horse came from outside on the drive, a door slammed below, and then she heard a servant taking the mount away to the barn. Darcourt, probably, she told herself. He had been missing from the supper table. From the remarks about his absence she gathered that there was nothing unusual in that. A while later she heard his footsteps in the hall as he went up to bed.

She had missed Darcourt, his laughing comments and the light of encouragement and conspiracy in his eyes. It would not do, however, to become too fond of him. There could be no future in it. But the time she had spent in the front parlor after supper had dragged amazingly.

Grand'mere had played at embroidery with a piece of linen, a tangle of silks in various shades of heliotrope, and a tambour frame. In a petulant mood she had insisted on a fire to warm her old bones and dispel the damp. Then she had hidden behind a three-legged firescreen stand of woven reeds to protect her face from the flames dancing on the hearth.

Bernard had been moody, with little to say even to Celestine, who practiced her wiles upon him quite openly.

"You must not mind my grandson, ma chère," Grand'mere had told the girl with a frosty smile. "He often forgets us for hours at a time when more weighty matters occupy his mind."

Bernard had thrown her an oblique glance but had not in any way changed his attitude. Finally tiring of trying to make conversation with him in his morose study of his booted feet, Celestine had turned her attention to Elizabeth.

By that time Elizabeth, for something to do, had taken the skeins of embroidery silks from the basket beside Grand'mere's chair to try and separate them. As Celestine sat down beside her she had to pick up a number of strands that the other girl had carelessly swept to the floor with a whirl of her full skirts, which were held out by one of the newly fashionable *crins,* or horsehair padded underskirts.

There had followed a catechism on Felix, his health, his clothes, his likes and dislikes. She had answered as best she could. It had not been hard, since she had lived in the same house with him for the few short weeks he had stayed with them. As often as not she had planned the meals that he ate and seen to it that the rooms occupied by the couple were as Felix wanted them. She had answered so easily and with such quiet composure that at last Celestine had flounced away in a pet.

For a second she had smiled in amused triumph, but then she had caught Bernard's dark gaze lingering on her mouth. The pleating on the bodice of her black bombazine had quivered with the sudden thudding of her heart; her fingers had clenched on the silk threads in her hands. Soon after, she had gone upstairs.

"Are you awake?"

Elizabeth sat up, pulling the sheet around her. The door to the hall was still without its key. She regretted not asking Grand'mere for it when she recognized the voice of Alma Delacroix. Without enthusiasm she called to her to come in.

"I can't sleep for the noise," said Madame Delacroix. "Oh, I know that it is quiet enough, but the sound of the crickets and the frogs on the bayou drives me distracted. It is so much worse this time of year. I prefer street noises, town noises. You hardly hear those. It's no use telling me that it's whatever you get used to, either. I'll never get used to the country!"

The woman carried a small candle. In its wavering light her face looked bloated and unnaturally pale but determined as she drew near the bed.

"I heard you tossing and turning in here while I waited for Darcourt, so I was sure you were not asleep either. Darcourt came to see me before he retired for the night. He is such a good son."

Elizabeth murmured something agreeable and moved her feet to one side to accommodate her unexpected visitor on the foot of the bed. Remembering the snub Alma had given her at the dinner table, she was suspicious of her

80

affability. She wondered whether Alma knew Bernard had seen her that afternoon, and whether this was the cause of Alma's sudden interest in her.

"You are very lucky then," she said, when she realized Alma was staring at her expectantly.

"Oh, yes, we have our difficulties, our differences, but we never forget, my son and I, that we have only each other. No one wants us here. I get a great deal of pleasure at times out of staying on while they wish me and my children to the devil. So you see, we have something in common."

Such unexpected forthrightness caught Elizabeth off guard. "Wht do you mean?" she stammered.

"Oh, please. Don't let's play games. You must know you are tolerated for the sake of your child. It has always been thus of me too, except I am tolerated because I was Gaspard's wife. Oh, I was very happy until he was killed. He was much like Bernard. He commanded respect for me from his sons, and even from the old lady, his mother. She would not have dared to use me then as she does now. Not that Gaspard and I always agreed. We did not. He wanted to treat Darcourt, my own dear heart, just as he did his own sons, Felix and Bernard. I could not have that, of course. Darcourt had never been disciplined so harshly. Besides, I suspected my poor Gaspard was jealous. Darcourt looks so exactly like his father, my first husband. He has his father's temperament, so many of his charming manners. You understand that I could not allow him to come completely under the power of my second husband. He was my own flesh and blood. I had to take his side. I know you understand this, the fullness of a mother's love. You have a son of your own."

"Yes, I see." Elizabeth said, but she was troubled. She did not understand why Alma was confiding in her. She was not sure that, in the way that confidences often do, the knowledge might not become a burden.

"I would do anything for my son, you know. Anything!"

Alma leaned forward, fixing her small dark eyes on Elizabeth's face, her voice quivering with intensity. Then as a whiff of the woman's breath, laden with brandy fumes, crossed the air between them, Elizabeth relaxed. She had been drinking. Relief made her giddy so that she nearly laughed aloud. She had not realized until then how unstrung she had been. With renewed confidence she set herself to reassure Alma, and to persuade her to return to her own room. She succeeded at last.

Alma, with her hand on the doorknob, turned back. "You are a nice girl, not at all a shy violet. Robust girls are not the fashion but a woman in fragile health can be so tiresome, not only to herself but to everyone around her. I know. I have never been in the best of health myself. We quite expected to have to wait on you hand and foot. Bernard had a stout woman chosen from the house servants whose sole duty was to have been to help you up and down the stairs. Isn't it amusing?"

"Yes, very."

"Well, goodnight."

The letters, it had to be the letters. Would she never get away from them? It did not seem so. As long as she remained in ignorance of just what Felix had written about his wife, she would be at the mercy of whoever had them.

Why had she not given more consideration to his letters? The answer was that she knew there could not be many, two or maybe four at the most. Felix had known his bride only two months altogether. And he was not the type to write long detailed accounts to his family.

But one letter could prove fatal. What a relief it would be to know exactly what Felix had written. Then she would know what to do, how to act or what to say to explain away any apparent difference.

Perhaps the letters had been destroyed. It was more than likely, she tried to tell herself. But what if they had not? What if Bernard or Grand'mere decided to read them again? What would they find?

There was no way of knowing. Or was there? If Grand'mere had letters they would be in her room or in the small sitting room where she attended to her correspondence. Bernard's would more than likely be in his desk in the library.

What else might be in the deep drawers of that great

desk? The marriage record and the Brewster family Bible had disappeared. Might they not also be in Bernard's desk? It was possible. Such an arrogant man would never dream that she would think of suspecting him, or that she would dare to search his property!

Thunder rolled nearer and lightning flashes came closer together as she cautiously approached the thought of what she intended to do. Could she do it? The sound of the storm would cover any noise she made. Suppose she were caught? She would say the storm had disturbed her and she had wanted to find something to read. That is, she would if she could manage to speak. Already she was trembling with fright. She would die of it if she were discovered.

Was it worth the effort? That was hard to say. It depended on what she found. If it meant the difference between staying here with Joseph in comfortable security, an accepted member of the Delacroix family, or being cast out as an imposter, someone with no claim to Joseph, the answer was yes, it was worth it.

Abruptly she threw back the covers, pushed her arms into her dressing gown and stood up. With her tossing and turning her usual long thick bedtime plait had come loose and she pushed the mass of auburn hair impatiently behind her shoulders as she tied the belt of her dressing gown. She found her slippers in the light of the lightning flashes. She had blown out her candle when she went to bed and she had no tinderbox with which to relight it. She would have to find a light downstairs.

There was no sound in the hall beyond the door as she stood listening, no movement as she pushed open the door and stepped out of her room with an assumed air of normalcy. The desire to run back inside and slam the door behind her nearly overwhelmed her, but she forced herself to move out into the open hall.

The hall was dark, lit only by the intermittent lightning. In its echoing space the sound of the wind outside seemed louder, more threatening. No sound came from the rooms with their tightly closed doors. That meant nothing, she told herself. There was a feeling in the air, a guardedness, a sense of tension, and she was not at all sure it came only from herself. It is the storm coming, she told herself, but she was not convinced.

She walked quietly, but without tiptoeing, to the stairs. She must not look furtive if she should happen to be seen. She held tight to the bannister as she descended, and the hand that caught at the skirt of her dressing gown to keep it from beneath her feet crushed the fabric. In the lower hall she looked back up the stairs, but there was nothing, no one, there.

The knob of the library door turned easily in her hand. She paused on the threshold, bracing herself, and then she stepped into the room and pushed the door quietly to behind herself.

As she moved forward lightning crackled across the sky beyond the window, glowing in the room. In its light she saw a white-faced woman moving toward her. She flinched and came to a halt before she realized she was seeing her own reflection in the black crepe-draped mirror over the fireplace mantle.

She pressed her lips together in irritation with her nervousness and went swiftly to the desk. Beside the whale oil lamp on the desk was an ornamental box of friction matches. Though she was unfamiliar with them, Elizabeth had seen them used. After several tries, a match spurted into flame for her with a shower of sparks.

She turned up the wick of the lamp and held the match to it, and then, as it caught, she blew out the match and threw the glowing stem into the fireplace. Carefully she adjusted the flame. The lamplight—in addition to the ordinary act of lighting the lamp—seemed to banish most of her fears as it brought the room into focus.

She put out her hand to touch one of the desk drawers, and then shook her head. Quickly she went to the bookcases and took down a novel, *Sense and Sensibility,* by the Englishwoman, Jane Austen. She brought it back and placed it on the desk top, and then began her search.

Though she tried to work quietly, pens and pen nibs rattled, and the rustling of the papers that filled the drawers was loud in her ears. She found account books stuffed with letters from the commission merchant in New Orleans, a plantation journal, legal documents neatly tied up with

84

ribbon, scribbled notes, and a sheaf of bills of lading and lists having to do with the transportation and storage of both cotton and sugar cane. But there was nothing personal in any of the drawers, and no letters from Felix. Sighing she pushed in the last drawer and straightened.

A small sound, like an indrawn breath, came from the doorway. Elizabeth froze. Seconds ticked past, marked with monotonous precision by the clock on one end of the mantle. She raised her head slowly to stare at the pale girl in the doorway. In the silence she noticed in some surprise that the storm was upon them and the rain had begun. It roared on the roof with a muffled drumming, and splashed on the gallery, blown under the overhanging roof by the wind. Thunder grumbled and the blue-white glare of the lightning flashes flickered into the room with a constant glow.

"What are you doing in here?"

The young voice was high and hysterical as Theresa took a step forward. Her eyes had a brightness that was more than anger, and her hands were clenched into fists at her sides. She wore a white nightgown that came to her ankles. The yoke and the cuffs that fell over her hands were made of soft outing material with lace.

"I—I was looking for a book." Elizabeth put her hand on the volume she had laid ready on the desk.

"In Bernard's desk? You must think I am stupid, like everyone else. You were looking for something. I saw you. What was it?"

Elizabeth smiled with an effort. "You are right, in a way. I thought I might find a bit of paper and a pen in case I did not care for the book."

"Didn't you find it?"

"Your—step-brother's papers do not run to the kind of stationery a female could use, I'm afraid." She forced a smile.

"It is an odd time to be writing letters." Theresa's voice was hard with disbelief.

"I was not at all sleepy. Storms keep me awake. I find them disturbing at times, don't you?"

A spasm crossed Theresa's thin face. "Why did you say that? You wanted to remind me! You want to upset me so you can send me away! We knew you would! We knew you would!" Her voice rising to a scream, she whirled, picked up a crystal vase, and threw it at Elizabeth.

She dodged instinctively, but the vase filled with purple wood violets flew wide to strike the mirror over the fireplace, splintering the glass. Water dripped from the mantle where violets lay in a puddle mingling with slivers of glittering mirror.

The noise and destruction seemed to fill Theresa with delight. She caught up a book from the small table near her and sent it spinning with pages flying toward Elizabeth. Swooping on another table she heaved a heavy wooden tobacco humidor that sprayed loose tobacco over the rug, then followed it with the collection of pipes, screaming with shrill passion. Then her eyes went to the heavy pewter lamp burning on the desk.

Elizabeth, retreating before the hail of pipes and rubbing her forearm where one had struck her, saw the direction of the demented gaze. She lunged toward the lamp, catching it up and holding it high above her head with both hands as she tried to put distance between Theresa and herself.

Enraged, Theresa stooped to pick up the heavy humidor from the floor, and threw it again. Elizabeth moved quickly aside and it flew through the window behind her with a tinkling crash of broken glass. Then the girl was upon her, clawing at her arms, her teeth bared in a grimace, trying to reach the lamp that swayed precariously above their heads in Elizabeth's grip. Elizabeth tried to fend her off with one hand, but in her hysteria the girl was as strong as she was.

The wet wind blowing in at the broken window sent Elizabeth's hair flying about her face, and whipped the lamp flame so that it leaped and flattened. Theresa got one hand on the base of the lamp, and they rocked back and forth, fighting for possession. As they tilted the lamp, the metal globe fell to the floor with a clang, exposing the flame.

Suddenly Theresa gave a shrill scream of pure terror. The frill of her long gown sleeve was on fire! She shook her arm, clawing at it with her free hand, spinning around in a frenzy of pain and fear.

86

For one long incredulous moment Elizabeth could only stare. Hastily she looked around for somewhere to put the lamp, finally setting it on the floor.

Even as she began to approach the girl she heard footsteps coming down the stairs. She tried to close in on Theresa, to catch her arm, telling her to be still, but Theresa pulled away, her eyes filled with unreasoning horror.

Bernard appeared in the door with Darcourt behind him. After one glance Bernard began to shrug out of his open dressing gown as he ran across the room.

Darcourt saw Bernard's purpose. "Let me," he said. "She will be more likely to let me."

They closed in on Theresa. Bernard caught her from behind and Darcourt wrapped the dressing gown around the burning sleeve, smothering the flames.

Theresa shrieked as she felt herself caught, and then some measure of sanity returned as she recognized her brother. She threw herself at him, collapsing against his chest as his arms closed around her.

"She did it, she did it, she did it," Theresa cried, hiding her face against him, and bursting into wracking sobs.

Elizabeth gasped. She had backed away to the broken window to get out of the way of the two men. As a safety precaution she had picked up the lamp from the floor, afraid they might kick it over. Now above the naked flame she met Bernard's accusing eyes.

The sound of the storm, the wind and the rain and thunder, seemed to engulf her with a roaring in her ears. The wind through the window whipped her hair into wild, red witch strands that hovered near the arrow of flame fluttering on the wick. The flame was wavering, she realized, staring at it dumbly, because of the weakness of her nerveless fingers. Her mind ceased to function for a long moment as she tried desperately to gather her wits to meet this new assault. How could she explain that Theresa had attacked her without saying why? How could she explain her presence? Even Theresa had not believed her excuses. And what could she say when Theresa told them she had been riffling the desk? There was a blackness hovering near the edge of her mind. It would be so easy to succumb to it, to let it solve her problems.

But pride would not let her take that cowardly retreat. With an extreme effort she forced her mind to clear. The effort left her empty, wrapped in a fatalistic calm. She did not resist as Bernard took the lamp from her and set it on the table behind him.

Darcourt unwrapped Theresa's arm and dropped the singed dressing gown to the floor. Swinging his sister up into his arms, he strode with her from the room. Elizabeth heard him begin to mount the stairs. The soft sound of Theresa's sobs seemed to linger in the room long after the sound of his footsteps had ceased.

Bernard sighed and looked down at her. Then, as if the sight of her pained him, he looked away.

"What in heaven's name were you doing down here on a night like this?"

He wore his nightshirt tucked into a pair of hastily donned pantaloons. The deep vee, the wide spread wings of his collar, and the full-gathered sleeves gave him the look of an ancient nobleman. His ruffled hair and his eyes, hooded with cynicism, added to this impression.

Elizabeth looked away. "A book—I couldn't sleep," she replied, a weariness in her voice that gave greater credence to the lie than anything else could have done.

"What—" he began, then he halted with an abrupt gesture of dismissal that somehow took in the lateness of the hour, her overwrought tiredness, and their improper attire.

"Never mind. Let me give you something to drink. A cognac, perhaps? Strictly medicinal, of course," he added as her eyes widened. Strong spirits never passed the lips of the well-bred lady.

"No, no. Please, all I want is to go to my room, if I may?"

"Very well. I will have a glass of madeira brought to your room. I expect you need something restorative."

"Th-thank you," she stammered. His concern with her well-being nonplussed her. She had expected something quite different. But if he was not going to detain her, then all she wanted was to escape, to return to the privacy of her room while she could still hold her nerves and emotions in check.

Bernard bowed her from the room, then blew out the

lamp guttering in the draft from the window and followed her.

At the top of the stairs Grand'mere stood waiting, her face an imperious mask. Elizabeth looked up as she neared her, but the stare of the old lady was fixed not on her but on Bernard. In that stare there seemed to be a questioning anxiety. She barely nodded as Elizabeth passed her, and then she began to descend the stairs.

Elizabeth rounded the newel post and crossed the hall to her room. Callie met her at the door. In the room beyond she could hear Joseph fretting.

"What happened down there, Mis' Ellen? What was all the screeching about?"

"Miss Theresa was upset, Callie. I don't know exactly why. There is something strange about that girl."

"Yes'm. I know what you talking about. They keep her too much to herself, if you ask me. I been wondering if she was sick somehow."

"So they say," Elizabeth answered dryly. The idea that had been forming in her head was sent flying by the sound of Joseph beginning to cry in earnest.

"What is the matter with him, Callie?"

"Oh, I clean forgot what I started out to do. I've used all the clean cloths Grand'mere laid out for diapers. I wanted to ask her which drawer to look in. I hate to just go plundering through the drawers of her big wardrobe—armoire, as she calls it. She wouldn't like it."

"I don't imagine she would. You go on and see to Joseph and I'll speak to Grand'mere about it."

"Yes'm."

Elizabeth turned back toward the stairs. She had her hand on the smooth wooden coil of the newel post when she heard Grand'mere speaking somewhere below.

"—half-child, half-witch, that girl. I won't have it, Bernard. She will have to go. I very nearly died when Joseph was found at the top of the stairs. She has killed once—"

"We don't know that."

"You won't believe it, you mean. Your father was as surefooted as a goat climbing a rail fence. Someone pushed him from the scaffolding of this house."

"Accidents happen."

"Don't tell me that. I've heard it too often, but I'll never believe it."

"Just because she is Alma's daughter—"

"Are you accusing me of prejudice? If so, I deny it. I have never pretended to like Alma, indeed, I fail to see how anyone could. She made my son's life a misery, and, even at her age when she should be putting on her dowager's cap and taking a chaperone's chair, she still ogles every personable man she meets! But that has nothing to do with her daughter. Oh, I'll admit she can be a likable child at times, but—"

"Child?"

"Girl then. But there has always been a wild strain in that family. Alma's own father was hand in glove with that pirate, Jean Lafitte."

"You should know. You never exactly turned that gentleman from your door."

"That was before 1812, while he was sailing under letters of marque. Even the governor's lady, Madame Caliborne, once had dinner with him at that time. I never entertained a pirate! But you are trying to distract me. I want you to send that girl away. I won't have her here. I won't, I tell you!"

"This is my house, and I will not have Theresa mistreated."

"Mistreated?"

"Yes, mistreated. We will guard against any further occurrences. That is my last word on the subject."

"You are a fool over that girl, Bernard. You always have been from the time you were in your teens and she little more than a baby. The men of this family have always been fools about women. Look at your father, marrying a woman like Alma when he should have been old enough to have more judgment. Then Felix celebrating his betrothal to one well-dowered *parti* then marrying an unknown chit without a penny within the month."

Elizabeth moved hurriedly away. She did not want to hear any more. She would have to find a diaper herself. *Half-child, half-witch—half-mad?* But just as Bernard was holding her at Oak Shade by her love for Joseph, he was also holding Theresa.

Why?

There had been that attempt to frighten her. Could it have been more than that? What if she had been bitten by the black widow? Then there had been the attack on Callie and the danger to Joseph. Suppose they had both died, who would have benefited?

Bernard. Perhaps that was why he kept Theresa near him. He wanted the poor mad thing to rid him of the two people who stood in his way. Or perhaps he needed her as a scapegoat!

"Why, what's the matter? Your skin is the color of milk, honey. I thought you was white awhile ago, but nothing like now."

"Oh, Callie. What is going to become of us?"

"Before I answer, you tell what's done happened. I know something ain't right."

Quickly Elizabeth told her. Callie's face took on the grim solidity of stone.

"We can't stay here," she said.

"We must. Bernard will not allow me to leave with Joseph."

"You could say that you wanted to—visit with some of your kin people, couldn't you? He might let you leave if he thought you were coming back."

"So soon after arriving? I doubt I could make him believe it after our clash today."

"Maybe if we was real careful, and waited a week or two?"

"It's possible," Elizabeth agreed slowly. "But we would have to make a show of being satisfied, and take extreme care."

"I see that. It wouldn't do to let him guess what we was planning. He'd stop us for sure."

"Oh, Callie. That isn't what I meant. We must watch Joseph night and day. We must think twice before we say every word. There is danger all around us. Someone tried to kill Joseph and make it look like an accident caused by your carelessness. Someone has tried, I'm convinced, to harm me. They were not successful, but the next time they may be less concerned with making it look like accidents or child-like malevolence and more concerned with results. It is obvious that the people in this house, even Grand'mere who professes to care so much for Joseph, are in league against us. Suppose they had reason to suspect that I am not Ellen. They would take legal action at the very—"

"Shhh, listen." Callie held a finger to her lips, her wide gaze on the door.

A discreet tap sounded on the panel. Elizabeth nodded to Callie, who moved to open the door with Joseph in the crook of her arm, his long gown trailing down the front of her apron.

Alma stood in the doorway, her face without expression as she stared past Callie. "Ah, Elizabeth, I hope you are all right?" she said, and then went on without waiting for an answer, "But it is Grand'mere that I need."

"She is downstairs," Elizabeth said.

"Then, if you have no objection, I would like to step inside. I have given Theresa a draught of laudanum for the pain of her burn, but it was not enough and I used the last of my own. I believe, however, that I know the shelf in the armoire that Grand'mere keeps her medicaments on."

"Yes, Alma?"

It was a relief to hear Grand'mere's aristocratic tones and to see her approaching from down the hall. The old lady quickly had the situation under control. The laudanum was brought out for Alma, a diaper found for Joseph, and Elizabeth, after drinking the wine sent up by Bernard, was ordered to bed.

But sleep could not be ordered and the first clear light of dawn was creeping around the edges of the drapes before her mind wore itself out with fears and speculation. She fell into a heavy slumber that gave no rest.

With the bright light of morning came a lessening of tension. The events of the night before took on a feeling of unreality. There was a lingering feeling of unease, of guardedness, but as the hours slipped by and no one mentioned what had happened, those terrible moments in the library faded. Elizabeth began to feel a renewed sense of confidence in the rightness of what she was doing and in her ability to carry it through.

It was during the afternoon siesta time that Denise

came to Elizabeth's room. Due to her sleepless night, Elizabeth had been taking advantage of the hours of repose. Her entire body was so heavy with exhaustion that it was some few minutes before she could get to the door.

"Would you come with me, *s'il vous plaît?* Madame Alma wishes to speak to you." There was something in the Frenchwoman's manner that jarred on her nerves, but glancing at herself in the small mirror set in the door of her armoire and smoothing a few ruffled hairs into place, she followed Denise along the hall.

Alma lay, *en déshabillé,* among the dingy lace pillows scattered over a chaise of the kind made popular by Pauline Bonaparte, Napoleon's notorious sister. Alma had been absent from the dinner table and it was obvious that she had scarcely moved from her position on the chaise all day. From the evidence, it appeared that most of her days were spent in much the same manner. A number of French novels, thin salacious volumes in yellow covers, lay among the pillows. A depleted box of bonbons lay on the floor. On a table nearby stood a collection of bottles and porcelain pots of rouge, kohl, and *maquillage,* that enamel-hard face-covering that cracked if the wearer dared to smile. A silver-backed hand mirror was flung carelessly among the cosmetics.

Elizabeth dragged her gaze from the table. Though she had never actually seen most of the things on it, she did not want to appear to be staring. No lady admitted to painting her face. The discreet application of rice powder papers to remove the shine from the forehead, nose and chin, and a whisk across the cheeks with either rose petals or the very daring red Spanish papers, were the only acceptable improvements on nature.

The light was dim, the drapes closed. Not a breath of air stirred. The stale odors of old perfume and hot wax from the candles burning in the girondole hung in the room, clinging to its tasteless clutter.

"You must forgive me if I don't get up. I feel quite done in. Emotional upsets are most fatiguing, don't you agree?" Alma said, as Elizabeth advanced into the room. Switching her gaze to Denise, she went on. "You have been most helpful, as always, my dear Denise. There is a bauble in

93

the box on my dressing table that you may have with my gratitude."

"Merci, oh merci, Madame—and Madame will not forget the other? You did promise, because of the message I—"

"No, I have not forgotten." Irritation laced Alma's voice. "You may give the order to the servants to move your bed into this room, but not just now, you understand?"

"Yes, Madame, of a certainty." Denise glanced at Elizabeth from the corner of her eyes, and then lowered her lids. Taking the piece of jewelry with her she left the room, but the careful manner in which she closed the door, shutting Elizabeth into the room with Alma, sent a tremor of apprehension along Elizabeth's nerves.

Alma stared after Denise, and then sighed. "Ah, well. I suppose it will be worth it. I do hate giving up my jewelry, poor bits that they are. But that is what one is reduced to when one is poor." She made a small careful movement of the lips, shrugging her plump shoulders under their satin morning wrap. Her hair, an unnatural deep black, was drawn to the top of her head in a severe, unbecoming style. In the candle gleam it had the hard repellent shine of the lacquer that kept it in place.

"To be poor is boring beyond anything, to be a widow also is to be sunk in ennui. I never would have credited it, but it is so, I assure you. You will understand in another year—when your grief has faded. Won't you?"

There was an odd lilt in her voice, something disturbing in the arch look in her black eyes that made Elizabeth wary.

"Perhaps."

"It occurred to me that Felix must have been very fond of you—and you of him, of course. My step-son had his father's excessive sense of responsibility, both of his sons do. It was oppressive at times, but such feelings are very worthwhile, especially when they result in generous portions for the unfortunate widows. My Gaspard left me very well provided for, unfortunately I never had the least

94

notion of economy. So I find myself with pockets to let. Mind you, I am not complaining. Still, I would not refuse if you felt able to lend me a little of the—er—ready?"

"I am very sorry, but I cannot help you." Elizabeth was unable to keep a certain stiffness out of her voice.

"Cannot? Or will not? The latter, I think. Let me put it to you bluntly. I know, for I have heard Bernard and the old lady talk of it, that you have a very comfortable allowance. I don't ask much, a few hundred, but I believe it will be in your best interests to see that I am not displeased. I could make it very unpleasant for you, I do assure you."

"Unpleasant? I don't know what you mean."

"I mean, *Chère,* that I have certain information about you and your precious sister that would upset your pony cart with a vengeance."

"My—my sister?"

"Dear Felix's wife!"

"You have been spying—" Elizabeth began, then the possible significance of the exchange of that piece of jewelry earlier struck her. "You must have paid Denise to spy on me!"

"Denise? That would be foolish beyond permission! No, the woman is useful to me as a message carrier, but despite the airs of intrigue she likes to give herself I do not tell her all I—discover." Alma's face cracked as a sneer curled her mouth. *"Oh, la vache!"* she muttered, snatching up her hand mirror to survey the damage to her mask of *maquillage*.

"Tell me," Elizabeth said, staring at the over-plump woman in her soiled wrapper. "Why haven't you gone to the others with what you know?"

"The others? What do I care about them? They have never liked me and make no bones about it. It makes no difference to me who takes their money, so long as I get my share. You think I like living here in this monument to the dead? Oh no, I have plans. There was a time, when Felix went away, that I hoped. I had persuaded him to make his will in favor of Darcourt, you see. Then he married your sister. That was a blow to the heart. Half a kingdom, for that was what it nearly was, gone." There was a stricken look on the ravaged face. Alma switched her gaze from the mirror back to Elizabeth.

"That is neither here nor there. Now I think you will be generous with me. After all, I was once in line for Queen Mother, and now you hold that place, however little right you may have to it. It should not be hard for you to spare a few pennies for my needs."

"I have no money, honestly."

"No, but you can get it."

Elizabeth ignored the sarcasm. "Not from Bernard. He as good as told me that I could expect nothing until I have proven that I am Ellen Marie Delacroix *née* Brewster. I cannot do that until I recover the things that were taken from my room."

"You have something of a problem then, don't you, *chère*? Well, I am in no great hurry. A week, two weeks, will serve just as well. But do not strain my patience too long. You might try a few wiles in the meantime. A few tears on Bernard's shoulder, beg him prettily, yes? You may be surprised how easy it will be to bring him around."

"I—I could not do that," Elizabeth said, her lips cold with fastidious horror at the idea of what Alma was implying.

She laughed, an unpleasant sound. "Why not? He is a man. You may be surprised also at what you can do—and how enjoyable it can be—when you must."

The image that Alma had evoked, the possibility of her going to Bernard and crying in his arms, stayed with her long after she had left his step-mother's room. Though she could not feature it happening, there was such a strange fascination in the thought that it was difficult for her to face Bernard with any degree of composure. She found herself avoiding his eyes, and barely speaking that night at the supper table. When she did force herself to smile at him the idea Alma had planted filled her brain and she could think of nothing sensible to say. She could only sit, crumbling a biscuit and sipping her sherry.

It was a relief when at last she could escape from the table to the small yellow sitting room beyond the great salon that was open only to visitors. Even though she had

96

to share it with Alma, Grand'mere and Celestine, she was at least free of the embarrassment of Bernard's presence.

Grand'mere took up her needlework. Celestine settled down beside her with a minute piece of embroidery, Bernard's initials surrounded by a laurel wreath. Alma, perhaps from the effect of six glasses of wine at the supper table, turned morose, complaining aloud in a whining voice. To keep from having to make conversation with her, Elizabeth wandered to the window, absently rubbing at the raw scratches made by Theresa's nails on her arms. The lamplight behind her made a mirror of the glass, so that the only thing visible in the outside darkness was the leaves of the trees, sparkling in the fitful moonlight, moving in the wind.

It was a rising wind, pushing before it dark masses of clouds that finally blotted out the moon. It had the feel of more rain. It was not a night for casual visitors, and yet Elizabeth thought she heard the sound of hooves on the gravel drive.

Soon the hammering of the great iron door knocker echoed through the house. Celestine rose, but Grand'mere frowned.

"Curiosity is unbecoming in a lady. If it concerns us Samson will inform us."

"What if it doesn't? Are you not curious at all about whoever it is?"

"It does not concern me," Grand'mere stated. But seeing Celestine's dissatisfaction, she relented. "It is an affair of total dullness, *ma chère*. Nothing at all mysterious. Merely the overseer from the Delacroix plantation adjoining this one, a man Bernard hired who has not been satisfactory. There is some question of misplaced funds, I believe."

"Oh." Boredom settled again over Celestine's fine, china-doll features.

The library door closed, so that they could no longer hear the murmur of voices. Although the subject seemed to be closed, Elizabeth could feel tension growing in the room. As the moments passed and no further sound came to indicate what was taking place, Alma began to fidget, picking at her cuticles and patting her hair. If Grand'mere or Celestine noticed, they did not show it, however; and Elizabeth was beginning to wonder if she was imagining things. Suddenly Alma surged to her feet.

"I'll return shortly," she said, moving toward the door.

"Where are you going?" Grand'mere asked in her blunt fashion, without looking up from her work.

"Upstairs," Alma replied, dropping her eyelids suggestively. "All that wine, at supper."

Grand'mere nodded, her face clearing. Alma glided from the room.

Alma's excuse was plausible, but Elizabeth did not believe it. When Grand'mere began a homily on self-control for ladies, Elizabeth waited until she had paused for breath and then murmured a plea to be excused, with the alibi of seeing about Joseph ready to her tongue in case she was challenged. When no one spoke, she slipped through the door and out into the hall. It was possible that she was being over-sensitive about Alma, but every movement the woman made was of interest to her. It had to be.

As she started toward the stairs, Bernard's valet, Ambrose, materialized from the dark regions of the house. He carried a large steaming can of hot water that he had heated in the kitchen wing at the rear of the house.

Ambrose stopped when he saw her, indicating with an inclination of his head that she was to precede him up the stairs. She went swiftly ahead of him so that he would not have to stand waiting with what she was sure was an awkward burden. "Have you seen Madame Alma?" she asked.

"No, Ma'am," he answered, "not since before supper. I saw her coming from the little white house down near the bayou then."

"Oh yes, thank you." Elizabeth said, remembering the day before when she had seen Alma near the pavilion herself.

"Yes, Ma'am." When they reached the top of the stairs, Ambrose walked steadily toward Bernard's bedroom. He looked as though the hot can he held by the handles with two white cloths was no more trouble than a silver card salver.

What now?

She had not intended to come upstairs, for she was almost certain that Alma had not done so. But Ambrose had obviously expected her to; she suspected he would have thought it strange if she did not. She could have no reason for wandering about the darkened rooms of the lower floor. The library was the only room other than the sitting room with a lighted lamp. Alma had not been so far ahead of her that she could have mounted the stairs and entered her room without Elizabeth seeing her. She might have slipped back into the dining room or the salon, but it did not seem likely since there was no apparent reason for it. Alma had not gone out the back; Elizabeth had Ambrose's word for it. That left the front door, and Elizabeth felt instinctively that this was the way Alma had gone.

Moving quickly but quietly, she went to the double doors which led out onto the gallery. She pulled one of them open, stepped out, and drew it shut behind her.

The night wind brushed her warm face with a chilling dampness. The sour tang of wet oak leaves was sharp in the dark. Beyond the edge of the gallery, a lantern hung from the ceiling of the lower floor, casting a yellow light which pushed feebly at the night blackness.

She paused to let her eyes adjust to the dark and then walked toward the railing and the light. She stopped while she herself was still in darkness, hidden from the ground by the stretch of gallery railing.

Clutching her forearms, she stared out at the windy night, wondering what had become of the early Southern spring she had heard so much about. Was it a myth, like miracles, and the handsome prince and happily-ever-after? She had come seeking the miracle of security and a little happiness, and all she had found was degradation and despair. Everything she did and said seemed to draw her deeper into this morass of lies. It was like quicksand—the more she struggled, the deeper she went.

Was she mad now, clutching at the proverbial straw, in thinking that Alma had something to hide, something that could be used against her to nullify her blackmail attempt? It seemed so. It seemed the height of lunacy to be standing out there in the darkness waiting for something, anything, to happen. And yet she had to make the effort. She could not give up without a fight. It was not her way.

Beneath her the front door slammed and she could hear the scuff of boot heels across the brick floor of the lower gallery. A horse, hitched to one of the rings set into the mounting block beside the front drive, lifted his head, jingling his bit and bridle and blowing softly through his nose.

Looking toward the sound, Elizabeth could just make out the shape of the horse on the far edge of the lantern's radius. Then the man, the overseer she assumed, came into view.

He was big; his broad shoulders strained the rough material of his shirt. The thick column of his neck, and the massive arms ending in wide hands with fingers like sausages, indicated brute strength. He clamped a hat on his mat of thick curls just as he reached his horse, and then he swept it off again as a woman glided toward him out of the shadows.

The light was dim but there could be no doubt. The woman was Alma. She drew close to him, speaking earnestly and placing one hand on his arm. He replied, bending his head, looking down at her. What were they saying? Elizabeth would have given much to know.

So intent was she on the scene below her that she did not hear the scrape of footsteps until they were directly behind her. Before she could turn she was caught. The warmth and strength of a man's arms, the smell of cigars and fresh linen enfolded her. He whispered against her hair as he drew her hard against him.

"Celestine, *ma coeur,* you waited."

CHAPTER 6

"Don't!" Elizabeth cried out, pressing her hands against his chest.

She was released immediately, but the damage was done. Alma and the man beside her raised pale, shocked faces toward the gallery, and then the overseer swung into his saddle and sent his horse galloping down the drive.

"My apologies," Darcourt said with stiff courtesy.

"You—you startled me," Elizabeth said, forcing a laugh. "But I expect you were more surprised than I."

"Yes." Relief that she was not offended was evident in his voice. "I needn't tell you that I expected someone else. Please forgive me?"

"Yes, do not think of it. Good night," she said, and sent him a smile across the darkness. She turned away and went back into the house.

The days, rainy and chilly, passed without any satisfaction from Alma. There had been no opportunity for Elizabeth to confront her with what she had seen, and Alma, knowing perhaps that it was to her advantage to avoid a confrontation, did nothing. Sometimes, however, Elizabeth caught Alma looking at her with such active dislike that she was filled with both satisfaction and a distinct uneasiness.

With the wet weather they were all confined to the house. There was little privacy, even in their bedrooms. Out of sheer boredom, each knew exactly where the others were at all times. No one was safe from interruption or eavesdropping. As a result, Callie and Elizabeth had stopped talking to each other except as mistress and maid. What had to be said was conveyed by a look or a nod.

Because the house was still in deep mourning they were spared the morning visits of friends and neighbors. Though they would have to come at some time, Elizabeth was thankful to be spared the ordeal just now. However, as the days of rain wore on she often thought that it might not be an entirely bad thing to have a visitor to take their minds off themselves.

Theresa's burns began to heal, but she was still confined to her room with what Grand'mere described as a *crise de nerfs,* nervous prostration. If Elizabeth suspected it was something more than that, she was unlikely to find out precisely what, for she was barred from the room as being unnecessarily upsetting to the injured girl. She had to depend for her news on the vague bulletins issued by Denise, Theresa's principal attendant.

For a time she had thought that she might be called to account in answer to the accusations that Theresa had made. Theresa had not yet told anyone that she had seen Elizabeth going through the desk. At last it began to be borne in on Elizabeth that what everyone wanted most was to forget what had happened. They wanted her to forget as well. The scratches on her arms faded, the window in the library was reglazed, and a painting replaced the broken mirror over the mantel. With the removal of these reminders the incident began to lose its clear taste of fear in her mind.

Through usage the house became familiar. Its grandeur ceased to be exceptional except at times when she was struck by the sight of a twenty-foot table laden with innumerable dishes, or a chandelier blazing with fifty wax candles at one time. Gradually she began to feel less constrained with the rest of the family, as well as the numerous servants who came and went. But a reserve remained. It was as if something held them all back, herself included, from anything other than day-to-day irritations and trivialities. Beneath the current of all conversations lay unspoken thoughts like snags waiting to founder the unwary in a moment of carelessness.

At last the weather cleared. The sun rose in a cloudless blue sky. Each blade of grass, each leaf, sparkled with rain jewels. The gravel on the drive glistened and birds sang, flitting among the trees around the house. The doors and windows were opened to the fresh sweet air so that those gathered at the breakfast table could see the change.

"What a lovely day to go to the chapel," Grand'mere said, a satisfied smile wrinkling her face in the clear light.

Bernard looked up from his plate. "Yes, of course," he said after a moment.

Alma's face took on a mutinous scowl, but she did not object. Darcourt and Celestine glanced at each other with a look of pained acceptance.

"Chapel?" Elizabeth asked finally, since she appeared to be the only one who needed to do so.

"Indeed, yes," Grand'mere answered. "We ordered a plaque, a memorial plaque for Felix, to be mounted in the family chapel. He may be lost to us, buried in some common grave—we may only hope in consecrated ground— but there must be some suitable remembrance, today of all days, the anniversary of his death."

It was true. Felix had died a year ago this day. Nervously Elizabeth fingered her mourning brooch, looking at her plate. She had forgotten.

Grand'mere went on. "The plaque is quite impressive, of bronze with a fitting sentiment engraved beneath the lettering. Bernard ordered the plaque in New Orleans last summer. It has been an unconscionable long time in arriving. Still, one cannot hurry artistry. Since it came so near the anniversary date, and also the time of your arrival, we felt that it would be a nice gesture to have it set in place today. All is in readiness. We even have a good omen. The rain has stopped."

"I see." What Elizabeth saw best was that this ceremony, if it could be called that, would be an ordeal. Would they expect her to be overcome with grief when confronted with the final evidence of Felix's death? Or could she carry through with a pretense of white-faced, courageous sorrow?

"You are very quiet," Grand'mere rapped out. "Don't you approve?"

103

Elizabeth nearly smiled. It still seemed strange that it should matter whether she approved or disapproved. "It sounds quite perfect. Tasteful and—fitting."

Alma snorted. "Tasteful? I should say it is tasteful. What else, pray? Also outrageously expensive."

"Mother," Darcourt said repressively.

"Don't use that tone with me, Darcourt. I will say what I please."

"Alma, have the goodness not to show such ill-breeding at my breakfast table." Grand'mere stared at her daughter-in-law.

"Ill-breeding!" Alma seemed to swell. "I am as good as anyone at this table, and a pox on stupid prohibitions against speaking of money. I suppose it is in keeping with the ostentation of that mausoleum built like a temple for the dead, but I think it is an amazingly expensive tribute when the same thing could have been chiseled into the marble, as was the name and date of my poor Gaspard. Especially at this time! Why, we are all having to stint ourselves. There are dozens of things we are told are too dear this year, such as our sojourn in France. It is too bad. Such a thing never happened while Gaspard was alive."

"Count yourself fortunate. You shared the good times with him. Felix and Bernard's mother, Amelie, was—"

"Grand'mere. Please?" Bernard interrupted the tirade.

"Very well. But I will hear no more on this subject. Alma, you may go to the chapel with us or not, just as you please. I don't believe you have been in some time."

At this veiled insinuation of a lack of respect and piety, argument threatened to break out again. But Darcourt rose and threw down his napkin, announcing his intention of going riding. Staring anxiously after her son, Alma let the comment pass.

Though the suggestion had been made at the breakfast table, it was well after dinner before it was acted upon. First Grand'mere had decided she must supervise the spring cleaning of her room. Then she had insisted on carrying Joseph with her to the ceremony, but she had not allowed anyone to awaken him from his afternoon nap.

"He will never remember a thing about it," Elizabeth had protested.

"Who can say what a baby will remember? Besides, he should be there. Felix was his father."

Elizabeth could not deny that, and so she was silent.

The family chapel stood some distance from the house. It was off the drive, near the main entrance gates from the road. Elizabeth elected to walk and Darcourt offered to escort her, whereupon Celestine joined them. Bernard was not able to come with them. Just after dinner he had had an emergency message from the plantation next to Oak Shade and had gone away with the messenger. Darcourt thought that it was about some missing equipment: "The overseer in charge over there probably sold it and pocketed the money. Bernard will straighten it out. He had better, he promised Grand'mere that he would join us at the chapel as soon as he could."

They walked three abreast, keeping to the drive to keep their feet dry. Before they were halfway down the drive, Grand'mere swept by in the carriage, Callie and Joseph inside with her and the liveried coachman on the seat.

Soon only the roof of the great house was visible behind them, shining in the westing sun. The curving of the drive, its slight downward grade, and the oaks, both those that lined the drive and those that stood sentinel on the lawn, hid it from them.

Except for an area just in front of the house, there had been no attempt to make a lawn. Beneath the tall oaks, the ground sloping to the road was free of tall weeds and scrub, but there was no formal grass. It was kept more in the nature of an English park. The leaves from the fall before were layered like brown sponge, and limbs blown down during the rains, some gray and rotting, some still with jaunty leaves waving bravely, were scattered under the spreading branches.

"Why did Alma decide not to come?" Celestine asked Darcourt as she clung to his arm. "Surely she didn't pay any attention to what Grand'mere said. Your mother knows what she is like!"

"Mother said that the quarrel brought on one of her migraine heads. She is lying in a darkened room with cologne compresses on her temples. Grand'mere knew it would bring one on—that is why the old lady provoked her. She didn't really want mother to come," said Darcourt.

"Why should she feel that way?" Elizabeth asked, from where she strolled on his right.

"Mother holds that Grand'mere dislikes everyone who is not a true Delacroix. She is positive that the old lady would be rid of her if she could find a pretext. Everyone knows that she was responsible for the death of the first wife, Amelie."

"That is not so." Celestine came to the defense of her distant relations. "Amelie was delicate. She never recovered her health after the birth of her sons."

"I won't argue the point, except to say that Grand'mere never allowed Amelie to pamper herself. She has never been ill a day in her life and so she never believed Amelie when she said she was not well, just as she never quite believes in Mother's headaches, and never allows the degree that she suffers from them."

"It must be distressing to your mother," Elizabeth commented.

"I wish I could take her away, so that she—and Theresa—would not have to endure the charity of the Delacroix."

Elizabeth did not know what to say, but Celestine was at no loss. With the confidence of long intimacy she exclaimed, "You, Darcourt? The way money runs through your fingers? Even if you could conjure up a fortune it would be gone in a twelve month."

He laughed, his good humor restored. "No doubt. And I have observed that people with fortunes are apt to acquire property, and people with property, like poor Bernard, spend a terrible amount of time and money trying to keep and increase it."

Celestine agreed, a gleam in her eye. "You would become unbearably dull, I have no doubt."

"I suppose then that the life of a *fainéant*—that is good-for-nothing to you, Ellen Marie—is for me. I would not want you to think me dull. So long as Bernard pays my debts and you continue to smile at me I see no reason for a fortune."

"No, but Bernard does not pay my debts—yet, and so money, and a lot of it, is still of interest to me."

"Is it? With your dowry?" A serious note had crept into Darcourt's voice.

Celestine nodded. "It certainly is. I have expensive tastes, as you well know."

"Oh, yes, I know. That is our trouble, bless your mercenary little soul, we know each other too well."

"Really, Darcourt!"

"Don't be coy, *chère*. We have no secrets from Ellen Marie, not since I mistook her for you in the dark a few nights ago." He grinned at Elizabeth across the top of Celestine's head, but from the corner of her eyes Celestine shot her a glance of pure dislike.

"Oh? And what happened?"

"Nothing that a girl with two men in her pocket need be jealous of," Darcourt answered.

This was not the first time Celestine had shown her dislike. Though there had been no open disagreement between them, the other girl never missed an opportunity to make Elizabeth feel that she was a usurper.

The thought had not occurred to her earlier, but after that exchange of intimate observations she found herself feeling like a gooseberry, an unwanted third, and she let the other two gain on her gradually until she walked behind them alone. Darcourt looked back once, his eyebrows raised in mock question. Then his teeth flashed white against the dark gold of his mustache as she shook her head and motioned for them to go on.

That Darcourt was in love with the beautiful Creole girl appeared obvious. That Celestine, whatever she might feel for Darcourt, was interested more in Bernard's wealth seemed equally plain. Elizabeth liked Darcourt. His shortcomings, so readily admitted that they seemed unimportant, were forgotten when he smiled or laughed. At times she felt that he used gaiety to cover his unhappiness, but it was only a passing thought that did not last under the sunny indifference of his shrug.

Some effort had been made to gravel the small path

from the drive to the chapel gleaming palely through the trees, but it had been wasted. The path was overgrown, and the gravel sunken into the soft, fertile earth. Weed rosettes supporting last year's dead brown stalks encroached on the path, and vines waved their new green shoots in the middle of the gravel, searching blindly for something to which to cling.

The coachman waited with the carriage where the path left the drive, but Grand'mere and Callie, carrying Joseph, had gone on. They stood impatiently beneath the cedar tree that stood with its feathery black shadow falling across the face of the small white chapel.

"Well! It's about time," Grand'mere greeted them. "You certainly dawdled along."

Digging one bony hand into her black string reticule, she took from it a large heavy key which she handed to Darcourt.

"I am certain I heard laughter, too. In my day one did not find an occasion such as this a time for levity. A widow was inconsolable, her grief unrestrained, her heart buried in the grave. She did not disport herself like an unmarried girl! A widow wore black until she remarried or died. My only son, Gaspard, has been dead a mere three years and already his wife speaks of going into purple, not that it matters since she is seldom out of her wrapper. Silly idiot, as if purple would be more becoming to her than black. And my grandson's widow running about the house in her dressing gown and giggling on the very anniversary of her husband's death like a debutante at her first night at the opera!" She continued to grumble in this vein as Darcourt fitted the key into the lock and pulled open the thick bronze doors.

Like the house and the small pavilion beside the bayou, the chapel was built along classic Greek lines, with a flat roof, a low entablature, and columns on three sides. It was, in fact, a miniature of the great house. It was built of brick, plastered over to protect it from the dampness, and painted white. A low iron fence, also painted white, enclosed a tiny, brick-floored terrace and the three shallow steps that led to the doors. On each of the two heavy bronze doors, a wreath flanked by two inverted torches stood out in relief. Beside the doors stood large grecian urns embraced by winged cherubs whose sightless eyes were fixed in an expression of melancholy.

The air inside the chapel was heavy with the smell of mildewed cloth and musty, faded flowers. Cobwebs in gray swaths were gathered in the corners of the high slits of windows, obscuring the already dim light that fell through the purple stained glass. Dust and grit grated beneath their feet on the dull white marble floor.

The walls fronting the burial vaults, as well as the ceiling, the small altar at the back, and even the reredos behind it, were all of the same white marble. Against its purity the white of the altar cloth was almost invisible, but the gold of the crucifix, vases, and candlesticks shone with a disturbing brightness.

Only one of the marble vaults was etched with lettering. It read: *Jean Marc Gaspard Delacroix, né le 23 Novembre 1794, décédé le 24 Juin 1834*

Beside it a brightly new bronze plaque had been fixed to the wall. The holes drilled for its placement had caused much of the grit underfoot. A shock ran over Elizabeth as she saw that the inscription was in English. She wondered if all those months ago Bernard had looked toward the possibility that Felix's wife might someday see it and appreciate the gesture. He could not have known that Ellen would be familiar with their language, her French-Creole mother's tongue. She found herself hoping that it was so in spite of the fact that Ellen would never see it.

In memory of Felix Gustave Joseph Delacroix, born 10 January 1809, died 17 March 1837, Goliad, Texas A man of valour. The inscription was simple, and yet it brought back to Elizabeth the memory of Felix as he had looked, darkly handsome, leaning down from his horse to tell Ellen goodbye. There had been a smile on his lips, but his eyes had been touched with understanding for the pain of being left behind.

Despite everything that had happened, Felix had been good for Ellen. They had loved each other; that was worth a great deal, and he had made her happy for a while. In the normal course of events, they would have lived out full lives together, and fifty years from now they would both be lying behind that cold marble front—but no, you could not say that. In the normal course of events they would never have met. As it was, they both lay in the warm soil of Texas.

Without realizing it she felt tears welling up behind her eyes. Grand'mere glanced at her from the corner of her shrewd old eyes and cleared her throat.

Before she could speak one of the heavy bronze doors swung inward with a small squeak of the hinges as Darcourt brushed against it.

Gasping, Celestine jumped. "I never fail," she exclaimed as they turned to look at her, "to imagine how terrible it would be to be shut up in here. I have a perfect horror of it!"

For once Grand'mere seemed to have exhausted her caustic observations. Celestine's nervous comment brought no answering retort. Instead Grand'mere turned fretful. "No one has been here for ages," she said. "It is Alma's duty to care for the chapel, but she has no taste for it. It is her fault that the cemetery and chapel are so far from the house. So inconvenient. She would have had it on the other side of the bayou if it had been left up to her. She's afraid of the dead, and of dying, or I miss my guess —you needn't stare at me, Darcourt. You know what she is like. I expect she even fears the ghosts of our Negro servants buried · under their white wooden markers behind this chapel!

"I'm getting too old for this, too stiff in my joints. Who will care for the dead when I am gone? Just look at this floor and the dead flowers. A disgrace! I am so glad none of my friends are here to see it. I would die of embarrassment."

"This here is a graveyard house?" Callie asked, her voice high as she broke an awed silence.

"Most assuredly," Grand'mere replied.

"You—you bake your dead people in them ovens, like bread?"

Celestine tittered and Grand'mere stared at her so that the girl put her slim, well-manicured hand over her mouth.

"No, no, of course not!" answered Grand'mere. "They are not ovens at all, you silly creature, though I can see,

110

now that you bring it to my attention, that the squares marked in the wall have somewhat the look of ovens. In this part of Louisiana we must bury our dear departed loved ones above the ground. You cannot dig a grave. We are below the sea level, is that not it, Darcourt? And the water is so near the top of the ground that at the depth of two or three feet the grave begins to fill with water."

"That's right," Darcourt agreed, with a wicked grin. "In the old days, the coffins floated out of the ground and fell apart, exposing the decaying bones of the corpse so that the dogs and wild animals could get at them."

"There is no need to be ghoulish," Grand'mere rapped, and taking pity on the wide-eyed nurse, sent her back to the carriage for the pail of water, cloths, brush broom and flowers for the altar.

"What Darcourt says is true, however," she went on to Elizabeth. "Everyone remarks on our peculiar burial customs, but they are dictated by necessity. Not everyone has their own private chapel, of course. In New Orleans they are building a wall of vaults six foot wide around the cemeteries. They look even more like ovens than this, I'm afraid. A most unfortunate, but not inaccurate, comparison. In the rural areas the vaults are made of bricks, or among the very poor and the slaves, the graves are piled with rocks, if they can find them. Ballast from the Northern ships is much in demand for that purpose."

When Callie returned, Grand'mere took Joseph into the crook of her arm and directed the cleaning with her cane while the baby stared up into her old face with a look of interested wonder.

They placed flags, the white iris, in the altar vases. When all was as perfect as the old lady could wish, she sent after the candle in its hurricane cover so that she could light the candles on the altar.

"Why didn't you bring a few of Bernard's friction matches?" Celestine asked. "It would have been much easier."

"New-fangled things like that are the devil's work. I will have no part of them. My grandmother and my mother always carried a candle to the chapel and so shall I."

"I couldn't do without them," Darcourt said, patting his waistcoat pocket, from which two cigars protruded. "I saw a peddler the other day who had matches in his pack. How about that? Bernard has been ordering them from Paris," he explained in response to Elizabeth's questioning look.

"Listen!"

They fell silent at Grand'mere's command, straining to hear. From the main road beyond the trees, the sound of a wagon could be heard. It seemed to be turning into the drive.

"It's Bernard. Darcourt, go and see. I did want all of us here. Tell Bernard to come at once."

"Bernard? In a wagon?" Darcourt asked.

"Well, of course not. But he may be riding beside it. Why else would a wagon be coming into the drive? In the ordinary way they would go on by the road around to the quarters." Her voice took on a strident note as if she felt she was dealing with fools.

Darcourt obeyed her, passing Callie as she came back with the candle flickering inside its glass globe. They questioned her but she had not seen the wagon, had not thought it worth looking back for since it meant she might drop the precious candle and earn Grand'mere's wrath. They stood waiting as patiently as they could until Darcourt returned.

"It was Bernard right enough. He wouldn't come back with me, however. He was taking the short cut to the hospital. There has been a little fracas. The overseer over in the next place had been lining his pockets at Bernard's expense, just as he thought. Bernard's valet, Ambrose, caught a ball in his shoulder. He must be in pretty bad shape, Bernard wanted him back here so he could keep an eye on him."

Grand'mere listened in silence, and then pressed her lips together. "There are women at the hospital to attend to wounds of that nature. Go after him at once, and tell him I desire his presence here."

Darcourt did not look hopeful, but he went away again. Again they stood waiting, for the most part, in silence. The sun sank lower in the sky and disappeared behind the trees. The shadows lengthened and the light in the chapel grew dim. The candle Callie had brought burned lower; soon it would go out. Joseph began to fret hungrily. Still Bernard did not come, nor did Darcourt return.

"Oh, very well," Grand'mere said at last. "We will proceed without them." Her voice boded ill for the two men when next she saw them.

She returned the baby to Callie's care. Then she took the candle from its hurricane shade, and, moving with a slow and ceremonial majesty, she lit the candles on the altar. With the ease of long practice she then crossed herself and knelt. Celestine knelt beside her.

Elizabeth looked at the irises, their white petals shimmering in the candle glow; she looked at the gold candlesticks, vases, and crucifix, which reflected the tongues of flame in their polished surfaces. It seemed in that moment that if she stood back she would always be alien to Oak Shade and its inhabitants, whereas there would be a kind of belonging in kneeling with them here in this place. Certainly there was more than enough reason for her to pray.

Slowly she crossed herself and sank to her knees, her full black skirts billowing around her.

At last Grand'mere sighed and rose to her feet. Elizabeth stood, and seeing Celestine trying to rise, hampered by her skirts, she gave her a hand to cling to while she got to her feet. The dark-haired girl accepted the proffered hand but gave no more than a perfunctory thank you before turning to Grand'mere.

"Oh, Grand'mere, *chère,* may I ride back in the carriage with you?" she asked winningly. "I am exhausted."

Grand'mere gave her assent, but not without a touch of scorn. "I suppose you want to squeeze in, too," she said, turning on Elizabeth.

After that remark Elizabeth felt she would not have ridden in the carriage even if she wanted to, which she did not. She welcomed the idea of the walk home in the dusk alone. She had been too much in the company of people in the last weeks. It would be a pleasure to have no one's company but her own.

She turned the key in the lock of the chapel door and handed it back to Grand'mere. Then she walked back out to the carriage on the drive with the other women.

She watched them drive away with something like gratitude. It was not until the sound of their going had faded and the silence of near night had fallen that she felt her first unease.

She tried to ignore it, to laugh at herself. After all, there was no danger. She knew who had tried to harm her and Joseph, didn't she?

To prove that she was afraid neither of shadows nor of the dark turnings of her own mind, she did not hurry toward the house. Instead she leaned against a tree, letting her mind roam, willing the peace of the close of day to invade her soul.

It was a relief to drop her pretense and be herself, without the need to appear the subdued and grieving widow. It had been a strain, she admitted to herself, expecially when cooped up in the house during the long days of rain and unseasonably cool weather. She had felt that everyone was watching her, weighing her performance, especially Bernard. It seemed that every time she looked up she found his dark inscrutable gaze upon her. But there had been no reference to the money, to his need of it, or to the lost papers that would secure it for her. She wished somehow that he would speak of it. His brooding silence on the subject was unnerving.

The noise of the crickets and other spring singing insects was loud in the woods around her. A night bird called mournfully. The wind touched the tops of the trees, swaying them gently. Regretfully she pushed away from the tree. Her footsteps as she started back toward the house in the thickening darkness were loud. She felt no better, there was no peace in her heart gained by her solitude. There seemed to be a barrier to peace within her mind. A barrier, she was afraid, of her own making, built of lies and deception.

CHAPTER 7

As she held her skirts above the clutch of the briars, she told herself firmly that though her role was a strain on her nerves, in some ways it was becoming easier. She often thought of herself as Ellen now. She answered to the name without effort. She took her place on Bernard's right at the table, and took her chair before the fireplace; she accepted as her due, accepted attention, the stool for her feet, the shawl for her shoulders, with a naturalness that was unfeigned. The idea of Felix's letters still disturbed her at times, but she had quietly searched Grand'mere's room and the small sitting room the old lady used for writing letters. Finding nothing, she had concluded that what few letters there had been must have been destroyed. The one other possibility was Bernard's bedroom, but if she were caught there it would be a more scandalous situation than she cared to contemplate. A young widow simply did not enter a bachelor's bedroom except under the most dire circumstances. There would be nothing she could offer in the way of an excuse, and after the ordeal in the library she could not bear to think of taking such a risk without some excuse with which to protect herself in case she was discovered.

As she neared one of the wide curves of the drive, she heard footsteps coming toward her. Bernard or Darcourt coming to escort her back to the house, she thought. Doubtless Grand'mere had not realized how close to full darkness it was when she left her behind, and her conscience had pricked her into asking someone to come and see about her.

Smiling a little, pleased at the sign of thoughtfulness, Elizabeth stopped. While she was waiting for whoever it was to come to her, she bent over to remove a brittle, dead briar that had caught on her skirt and broken off. But as she came to a halt the footsteps halted also.

She listened for a moment. "Bernard?" she called. "Darcourt?"

There was no answer.

"Darcourt?" she called again, a threatening note in her voice as it occurred to her that it would not be beyond him to have a bit of fun at her expense. She tried to peer through the low hanging limbs but she could see nothing except darkness beyond a few feet.

When there was still no answer she began to wonder if perhaps Theresa had given Denise the slip and had gotten out of the house. She shivered a little, and, taking a hold on her fancies, opened her mouth to call out again. But then she abruptly closed it when she remembered the overseer who had been dismissed, and the fracas which Darcourt had mentioned in such an offhand way but which had ended in bloodshed.

Suppose the overseer had resented his dismissal enough to come prowling about the big house looking for some way to get back at the people in it? He might think she would make as good a target for his revenge as any other. Or perhaps he was looking for Alma. He might object violently to anyone else becoming aware of his presence.

Before the thought had completely formed in her mind, she had stepped as quietly as possible off the road. The deep grass and dead leaves under the trees deadened the sound of her footsteps. She would wait to see who it was.

Minutes passed. Dew had fallen upon her so that her clothes were damp to the touch. A sense of coldness crept over her and she clutched her upper arms, feeling the chill bumps of fear through the thin bombazine of her sleeves. Her eyes burned from straining to see through the darkness.

Suddenly there was a small sound behind her of cloth rustling, and before she could move something soft and

116

clinging descended over her head and tightened around her throat. She caught at it, twisting and turning, digging her fingers under the rope of twisted cloth. Her breath rasped painfully in her throat, sending waves of panic to her brain. Her eyes throbbed with the beat of her heart.

She staggered back. Feeling her assailant behind her, she stepped down hard with her wooden-heeled walking shoes and threw her weight backward.

They went down together. Elizabeth felt the back of her head come in contact with a ridge of facial bone, and at the same time the constriction around her neck loosened. She rolled away, dragging air into her lungs in a sharp, audible gasp. Scrambling to her feet she started to run, but her skirt was caught and she plunged back to the ground. Desperately she rolled away from the grasping hands. She felt her sleeve rip and the cool air touch the bare skin of her arm. Then as her elbow came down on a fallen tree branch a shaft of pure rage struck through her terror.

She grasped the branch with both hands, rose to her knees and struck out, swinging it wildly. As she felt it thud against yielding flesh a cry of satisfaction sprang to her lips, and then she was up and running, her skirts clutched in both hands.

She dodged among the trees, ducking under the limbs, avoiding collision with them more by instinct than by sight. When she felt gravel under her feet she checked, but she knew that with her confining petticoats and skirt she would be a much easier quarry on the open drive than among the trees where she could hide. She was still too far from the house for a scream to be heard. Behind her she could hear the floundering sound of pursuit. Clenching her teeth together she crossed the road and ran into the trees. It was very hard to do this, with the drive beckoning toward the safety of the house, but she promised herself that she would double back toward it as soon as she safely could.

She ran, trying to put as much distance as she could between herself and her pursuer. She felt the pins leaving her hair and the heavy coil sliding down, spreading out over her shoulders. Her heart pounded in her chest with a harsh ache. Her breathing became labored, a stitch developed in her side and more than once she stumbled as the long dead grass threatened to trip her heavy feet.

At last she slowed and then stopped, reaching out to an oak for support, and then turned to lean with her back against it. Her ribs strained against her tight lacing for air, and she tried to quiet her harsh breathing to listen.

She could hear nothing. Had he given up, or was he standing quietly, listening for her, waiting to creep up on her again?

She shivered a little at the thought, pressing closer against the rough bark of the tree. Silence descended, an unnatural silence without the sound of insects or night birds. Her breathing slowed, her heartbeat steadied, but panic still hovered at the back of her mind. Her hands trembled and she had to clamp her jaws together to keep her teeth from chattering.

Drifting on the night air came a sweet, haunting fragrance. She turned her head to locate the direction from which it came, a mundane action to take her mind from her terror. At that moment something cracked with a sharp report behind her. She pushed away from the tree, running before she was three steps from it. A half dozen steps more and she had plunged into the thorny depths of that tantalizing fragrance, which had been coming from a thicket of mock orange.

She cried out, a short scream of pain quickly stifled, and then went still, She was caught like a rabbit in a snare, impaled on the long, sharp, green thorns of the mock orange trees.

It was difficult to move without noise, impossible to move without hurting herself further, but she tried. The effort started blood trickling from the scratches and small wounds on her bare arms and in her side, and it made her aware of the sickening numbness, as if she had been poisoned, where the thorns had entered the skin. A wave of dizziness rose to her head and she shuddered, and then she went on trembling uncontrollably. She could not stop the shudders that shook her, and she was unable to move when she heard the crashing of footsteps coming toward her.

"Ellen!"

She jumped then gasped with pain as the name rang through the night.

"Ellen?"

Bernard. Should she answer? If he was the one who had tried to kill her would he call her like that, encouraging the lamb to the slaughter? She stood still. When had she accepted, even subconsciously, that he could be her assailant?

Abruptly she called out. "Here." Then she called again, louder this time. If it had been Bernard it would not matter—but she did not, could not, finish the thought.

He was with her in a moment. Ruthlessly he pushed down the small orange trees and pulled her toward him. Then he let them snap back into place behind her. She tumbled, swaying against him.

"You are trembling," he said, holding her arms. "What in God's name were you doing?"

She tried to tell him but her voice shook so that she was not sure that he understood. Without commenting he stripped off his coat, wrapped it around her shoulders, and picked her up in his arms. Almost immediately they were surrounded by a search party made up of the butler, Samson, carrying a lantern, and two or three of the other menservants. At the sight of them, something flickered in her brain, but she was too distraught to catch the implication.

As he strode toward the house along the wagon track with the others following behind, she could feel the beat of his heart beneath his tucked shirt front. The smell of smoke from his pipe clung to the coat around her, and she was grateful that it had retained some of the warmth of his body heat. But there was little comfort in his arms. Their grip about her was hard with what seemed to be suppressed anger. Tears rose in a hard knot in her tight throat but she could not afford the comfort of release. Somehow she felt it was not yet safe.

Her trembling had begun to subside and a measure of composure had returned by the time they reached the lamplight pouring through the front door.

"You found her!" Grand'mere cried, coming toward them across the brightly lighted hall. "I would never have forgiven myself for leaving her if—"

119

"Then why did you?" Bernard interrupted her with a strange quietness.

"Why? She refused to come in the landau. Ask her yourself."

"I shall," he answered grimly over his shoulder as he mounted the stairs.

"I can walk," Elizabeth said, but her protest lacked conviction. It was just as well, since he ignored it.

Callie held open the door of Elizabeth's room for them to pass.

"Brandy—no, madeira," Bernard said to her.

She nodded and hurried away.

He put Elizabeth on the bed, not ungently.

Grand'mere followed him into the room, breathing a little quickly from mounting the stairs at such a fast pace. "You are very mysterious, Bernard. Is such solicitious care necessary?"

"Yes, unfortunately."

"I hope you mean to explain yourself," the old lady said, a dangerous edge to her voice, "for I warn you, I am tiring of these short answers."

Bernard turned to her and with an almost brutal economy of words told her what had happened. Elizabeth, listening carefully, could not think that he had left out any detail of what she had told him so hysterically. Perhaps he knew what had happened because he was there, her mind whispered, but she pushed the thought away.

"It is insane!" Grand'mere exclaimed. "Impossible. It could not have happened."

' "It did happen. Here, on these grounds. Under our very noses." A harsh anger grated in his voice, and Elizabeth had the irrational feeling that it was directed at her.

"Please," she murmured, but no one heard her. Opening her eyes, she watched as Bernard stared down at his grandmother.

The old lady twisted her hands together silently for a moment, and then she said in a small voice, "The overseer?"

Bernard said nothing. A shade of contempt crossed his face, though whether it was for the man or for the idea of his being the attacker could not be said. He turned suddenly and left the room.

When Callie returned, the two women helped her out of Bernard's coat. They exclaimed in horror at the patches of blood darkening her dress where the thorns had pierced the skin. But they averted their eyes from the torn sleeve, not in modesty but in an effort to gloss over that moment of terror.

Her injuries had been bathed and dressed, she had been helped into her nightgown and she had eaten the supper brought to her on a tray when Grand'mere came to her with a small dose of laudanum and persuaded her to take it. So beneficial for repairing the nerves, she said. She often took a little as insurance against a sleepless night, the bane of old age. The draught, administered in a little wine, was bitter, and Elizabeth made a face as she handed the glass back.

"I know," Grand'mere sympathized. "Bernard wants to ask you a few questions now, if you feel quite up to it. I don't at all approve—oh, not that he should visit you in your bedchamber, it was quite the thing in Paris in my youth for a lady to entertain her gentlemen friends while dressing—it should be quite unexceptional now in my presence—but I cannot think you should be plagued with questions."

"I don't mind," Elizabeth said, and was surprised at how weak her voice was. "I am not an invalid," she said a little louder.

"No, no," Grand'mere murmured and went away.

Elizabeth's eyes closed. When she opened them again, Bernard was standing beside the bed.

"I said," he repeated himself, "is there anything you can remember about the man who attacked you that would identify him?"

She frowned. "No. It was dark and there was no time. He was behind me."

"He?"

"The man. There were no skirts when I stepped back against him. It must have been a man."

"Could it have been a woman without skirts or petticoats?"

121

"I—I suppose. But she would have had to be very strong." Her eyes would not stay open in the bright light of the lamp left on the bedside table.

"Yet you got away from a strangle hold."

She smiled. "I am strong too."

"Are you?" There was a mocking humor in his voice that made Elizabeth wonder if she was not bordering on tipsy from the wine and then the laudanum. It was several moments before she realized that he had gone.

He seemed some distance away when he spoke again and she knew instinctively he was not speaking to her. "Where is Darcourt?" he asked from somewhere near the connecting door.

"The same place as always," Grand'mere answered with asperity. "A cock fight, a gambling hall, a bull baiting. I haven't seen him since I sent him after you. Typical, I suppose. He must have known you would not come and did not care to face me with it. He was never one for unpleasantness."

"And Theresa?" he questioned, ignoring the implication behind her words. "Can you trust that woman to be truthful with you? Can you swear that she has not been out of Denise's sight all evening?"

Instead of answering the question, Grand'mere asked in disbelief, "My dear boy, are you holding me responsible for this?"

The sound of the door opening came before Bernard spoke again. "Who else?"

Their footsteps receded and the door closed, cutting off the sound of their voices. Slowly Elizabeth opened her eyes. Grand'mere? It had been she who had arranged for her to walk home alone. The old lady was frail, but what was to keep her from hiring someone to rid herself of her unwanted guest so that she and her grandson could have full control of Joseph and his estate? Theresa, Alma, Grand'mere, Bernard. Who *was* responsible for that cloth that had tightened around her neck?

Something important tugged at her mind, something in the room. She let her gaze wander over the walls to the lamp left burning beside the bed, to the mosquito netting

ooped in the top of the canopy over the tall four posters
around her. Then she saw it.

Bernard's coat lay across the chair sitting against the
wall. Bernard's coat that he had wrapped about her, his
coat stained with her blood—and with mud.

She stared at the coat, remembering that terrible struggle on the wet ground, remembering that Bernard had
found her in the mock orange thicket with a search party
on his heels. What else could he have done but play the
gallant rescuer?

At last her vision began to blur. She felt herself sinking
into the mists of sleep. Panic seized her and she tried to
raise herself to escape the enveloping blackness. She was
afraid with the primitive fear she had known under the
oaks in the dark. How did she know it was only laudanum
Grand'mere had persuaded her to drink? How could she
be sure it was not some kind of poison? Whom could she
trust?

No one, she answered herself.

Dark waves of blackness closed over her head.

CHAPTER 8

Breakfast was brought to Elizabeth in bed the next morning, a simple French breakfast of coffee, hot crusty croissants, butter, and, as a concession to country life, dewber-
ry jam. She was still eating when Celestine knocked and
entered.

Celestine was beautiful and incredibly fragile-looking
in a lavender dress with huge drooping puffs of lace for

sleeves and a pansy purple velvet ribbon at her tiny waist. The effect was marred, however, by the straight line of her small mouth and the frown between her eyes. She asked Elizabeth how she was feeling and then she hardly listened to her reply.

Celestine had made it obvious that she felt superior in station, that she regarded Elizabeth as a poor relation with a questionable right to the hospitality she was receiving. Still, Elizabeth was surprised at the vehemence in her voice as she spoke.

"Well! Breakfast in bed. Receiving a surfeit of attention after your accident, are you not?"

"Everyone has been very kind, yes," Elizabeth said cautiously. It was not difficult to see that Celestine had something pressing on her mind.

"Kind? You must be delirious with joy at their kindness. You have tried in every possible way since you have been here to make yourself the center of attention, an object of concern. You think you can use their concern to insinuate yourself into their regard. You are, no doubt, good at that. You managed to attract Felix with your wiles."

"What?" Elizabeth could not believe what she was hearing. She had no idea that Celestine felt so strongly about her.

"Oh, yes. You are intelligent, I'm willing to grant you that. You know quite well that your suffering air and pathetic dignity will go down well with Grand'mere and Felix's brother—especially his brother. What did you use to capture Felix's attention? A tale of woe? He was always a fool for the downtrodden, a victim of knight errantry. No doubt you allowed him to think he was rescuing a maiden in distress."

"I am beginning to find this conversation distasteful," Elizabeth said quietly.

"Are you? That doesn't cause me great distress. There is much about you I have found distasteful from the moment you arrived. I have loathed having to stay under the same roof with you, having to look at you and know you are the cause of the greatest humiliation I have ever known. I have hated smiling and being pleasant to you. I find you extremely distasteful with your coy smiles at Bernard. You would smile less, I think, if you realized what he thinks of a brazen creature like you, the kind of female who would entice away a man betrothed to another. To us the betrothal is very nearly as sacred as the marriage, and to break it is unheard of, immoral."

"You feel, in fact, like a deserted wife?" Elizabeth asked, a curious note in her voice.

But the sound of her voice seemed to enrage Celestine further. "Now you cast about you for a substitute for Felix, and you think to have Bernard! You will not have him. He is a man of honor, of integrity. He will marry no one but me who has been dishonored by his family."

Elizabeth nearly laughed. If Celestine only knew how little use she, Elizabeth, had for Bernard as a husband, or any man for that matter. It was impossible for her to marry Bernard. Her chastity was an insurmountable barrier to a union with a man who thought she was a widow and the mother of a child. She knew she could never marry Bernard, but she was curious about him and his relationship with Celestine.

"Bernard will marry you—and you will accept him—simply because you were jilted by Felix?"

An alarming tide of color swept into Celestine's face. "You are unbearably insolent! How dare you say that to me? Bernard will marry me because he cares for me and because he wishes it. You have no conception of our code or our culture. This marriage will take place in spite of you and your machinations. You will do well to heed what I say. In fact it would be best for you if you went away. Everyone would be much happier."

"Oh, I couldn't do that," Elizabeth said. She was gaining a certain amount of satisfaction out of the fact that she was able to remain cool in the face of Celestine's insults.

"And why not?"

"I could not possibly leave without Joseph, and Bernard has refused to let him go."

Celestine stared at her. "Yes, of course. He would do that." A thoughtful look crossed her face.

A knock came at the door, and hard on the sound Callie walked into the room, a scowl between her eyes. She left the door open behind her.

"Is you through with your breakfast, honey? If you is think maybe you ought to rest awhile." Callie glanced a Celestine suggestively.

Celestine stared, opened her mouth as if to vent he anger on the Negro woman, and then spun around an went out the door, closing it behind her with a bang.

Elizabeth was preoccupied as Callie fussed around the bed, removing the tray, straightening the cover and fluff ing the pillows. She had the feeling that there was some thing unfinished between the two of them. Something im portant.

Callie stopped what she was doing and stood holding dressing gown in her work-worn hands. Elizabeth turne to her inquiringly.

"That lady don't seem to like you much."

"No, I don't think she does."

"And she's not the only one neither. We done had to many accidents, too many crazy things going on. Don' you think it's time we was getting out of here?"

"We can't, Callie."

"Why not, Mis' E—Ellen. This place ain't safe. We gonna be murdered in our beds. I ain't slept with two eye shut since we been here."

"I know," Elizabeth answered, plucking at a loose thread in the quilt over her knees. "But Bernard is Jo seph's guardian. He told me that if I go I can't take Joseph with me."

"Can he do that?" Callie demanded.

"I suppose he can. I don't know. But the legality of it doesn't matter. Out here in the middle of nowhere he could prevent me taking him by force if I tried to defy him. I confess that is what worries me more than the legal aspect. But Callie, where would we go? What would we do? I used the last of the bank draft Grand'mere sent for material for proper mourning clothes and our stage fare. There is not enough left to keep us more than a day or two in a town."

Callie was silent for a long moment. "You could hire me out as a washerwoman or to a hotel for a chamber- maid. Or sell me."

"Oh, no. You know I couldn't do that. We have been

126

through too much together. Besides, who would take care of Joseph?"

"You could get by," Callie insisted doggedly. "He could be weaned. He'd make it with milk to suck on a rag."

"It isn't necessary, Callie." Then she added to convince her, "Anyway, Bernard says you are no longer mine to sell. You belong to Joseph now—and Bernard has control of everything that belongs to Joseph."

The Negro woman's face paled and her eyes widened. "You mean that man could sell me, whenever he gets ready? Sell me away from you and my sweet baby Joseph?"

As she heard the anguish in Callie's voice, Elizabeth wished that she had never spoken. What good did it do for Callie to know that her fate rested with an indifferent master, one who had no understanding of her worth, one who did not care how she felt?

"I don't know Callie," she said unhappily. "That is the way it has to be as long as I pretend to be Ellen. Strictly speaking you don't really belong to me either, you know, but to that man back in Texas who foreclosed on our mortgage. Once Bernard started inquiring into it he might discover that, and then I suppose he could send you back. No, I think our best course is to go on as we started and see what happens. There is some money, twenty thousand dollars, that Felix left as a kind of widow's portion for Ellen."

"Lord, that's a lot of money."

"Yes, if we ever see any of it," Elizabeth agreed wryly, and went on. "But if worse comes to worst we might get away. Once we are away from the plantation we could go to New Orleans. We could lose ourselves in a large town like that. The hard part would be getting away from the vicinity of Oak Shade without being overtaken."

"We could! I know we could."

"But that is so hazardous, Callie, especially with Joseph. Just think how much worse off we would be if we were caught and brought back. There is no way of knowing what action Bernard might take. No, we must stay here and wait and see, at least until the money is ours." She was thoughtful a moment, and then she smiled wearily. "It is strange, isn't it, that I have very little more independence than you?"

Callie did not answer. She took a deep breath and let it out in a long sigh.

"Don't fall into a fit of dismals now, Callie," she said, reaching out to pat the other woman's hand, trying to infuse some humor, and with it some hope and confidence, into her voice. "We will be fine. We made it before and we will this time. I won't let anything happen to you."

"No'm, I know you won't," Callie said with simplicity.

Elizabeth kept to her bed the rest of the day. She played with Joseph, propping him up on her raised knees in bed, making him coo and gurgle, and kissing the tender softness of his neck. It was a warm spring day. The windows stood open to the gentle sun and the fresh flower-scented breeze lifted the lace curtains. The soft rustle of the new leaves on the oaks mingled with the calls of the birds, bringing a nebulous sense of relaxation. Despite the bruises or her body, the scratches and wounds from the thorns, Elizabeth felt a drowsy contentment induced entirely by the season. She tried to think, to decide what she was going to do, because it seemed that this state of affairs could not go on indefinitely. But her thoughts turned in circles without reaching any conclusions. In the afternoon, when Joseph fell asleep in the curve of her arm, she found herself yawning and her eyes began to grow heavy. She let herself drift into sleep, one arm around the baby, the other flung above her head.

She came awake abruptly, aware of a strong feeling of being watched. Turning her head slowly so as not to wake the sleeping baby, she saw that a draught from the window had caused the door into the hall to swing open. In the doorway stood Bernard.

He looked as if he had just come from the fields. Mud caked the soft leather riding boots that reached his knees and spotted his buckskin pantaloons. His white linen shirt was open to the waist, revealing the brown column of his throat and the silver medal shining against his chest. In his
128

hand he held his broad-brimmed, cream-colored planter's hat and his brown silk cravat. He appeared hot and weary. Lines of tiredness were cut into his face beside his mouth, and his hair, ruffled and disordered by the wind, fell forward onto his forehead.

There was a regretful look in his eyes as he met her gaze across the room. She stared at him, waiting with a strange breathlessness for him to speak. He turned on his heel and walked away.

For a long time Elizabeth lay gazing at the place where he had stood, disquiet gathering behind her eyes. What had brought that expression into his face? What did he have to regret? Was it something he had done, or something he intended to do?

Shivering a little, she drew Joseph closer to her and banished the image of Bernard's face from her mind.

Like most people who are usually healthy, Elizabeth soon tired of the confinement of the bed and her one small room. Even with Joseph's company, the evening stretched long before her. Grand'mere brought up books for her from the library, but since they were of Grand'mere's choosing, mostly sermons and parables designed to build character, they soon palled. She felt that she would lose some of the stiff soreness of her muscles and scratches if she could move about. She was restless and bored, her nerves increasingly on edge, and since she had taken the nap in the afternoon she was certain she would never be able to sleep. But though she chafed and complained laughingly, she was forced to give in when Callie deserted her side to agree with Grand'mere that she should not get up.

Her supper tray, designed to tempt her from moroseness, took up an hour or more. As she ate, she let Joseph taste things, laughing at his concentration as he tried to maneuver a tasty chop bone into his greedy little mouth. But at last Callie came and took the baby away to his bed. The tray was removed and she was refreshed with a sponge bath and fresh dressings for her injuries. Callie brushed her hair, bringing out the highlights in the russet

strands. The attention was supposed to bring about a feeling of repose, but it failed. Elizabeth was no nearer t
sleep when Callie finished than when she had begun.

"You all right, Mis' Ellen?" Callie asked as she stood a
the door about to leave the room.

"Oh, Callie, I'm afraid. None of this would have hap
pened if I hadn't come here."

"But you did come, and I been thinking you was righ
Now you got to finish what you started. This ain't no tim
to get chicken-hearted."

"I could tell them who I really am."

"Sure you could, but you can't expect them to love yo
for it. Nobody likes to be made a fool of like that. They'
show you the door for sure, and then who will take care o
Joseph and me? Who is to know what might happen to u
in this house with you gone? They ain't caring much now
how much you think they going to mind about us if yo
not around?"

Elizabeth nodded, sighing, but she did not reply.

Taking the action for a dismissal, Callie went on int
the room she shared with Joseph and Grand'mere an
shut the door.

Was Callie right? Would it increase the danger to Jo
seph and Callie if she were to have to leave them? Sh
thought again of the cloth scarf tightening around her ow
throat and the warm, sweet tenderness of Joseph's smal
neck. Could anyone do such a thing to a baby? Woul
they? The thought was not to be borne. In agitation sh
moved about the room.

The window was tightly closed against the noxious va-
pors of the night, according to Grand'mere's wishes, and
the drapes were pulled across the thin lace curtains. The
room felt stuffy, the air heavy with the smell of melting
wax and burning wick from the single candle. Longing for
a breath of air, Elizabeth put her hand on the drapes to
fling them back, but then she stopped. There was a certain
impression of safety behind the shielding drapes and fragile glass panes.

A shiver passed over her, and she hurriedly overlapped
the edges of the drapes where a crack of dim light could
be seen. Still the sound of the night penetrated, the spring

chorus of crickets and katy-dids and peeper frogs mingling with the deeper bass of bullfrogs on the bayou behind the house. Always before the sounds had been welcome, a part of the season, but now they only reinforced the impression that the night was alive with things unseen, crawling with menace. But was the menace outside? Could it not be closed inside the house with her?

Giving herself a mental shake for letting such disturbing thoughts into her mind, she turned away from the window —and saw Theresa.

The girl stood in the doorway, one hand still on the knob. She was dressed in her gown covered by a dressing gown of faded black velvet, a cast-off of her mother's, judging from the way the folds were wrapped about her frail body.

Theresa gave her head a toss, throwing the heavy plait of dark hair behind her back. The gesture had a hauteur about it that, with the vulnerable look in her eyes, was oddly touching. It reminded Elizabeth of the first time she had seen the girl outside her room trying to blend in with the shadows, a pathetic figure. The memory was preferable to that other of screaming hysteria. It gave her the composure to greet the girl quietly.

"They told me you were hurt," Theresa blurted out, without returning the greeting.

"Yes, but it was nothing serious."

"Then why have you been in bed all day?" The question came with disturbing swiftness.

"I think everyone thought I needed the rest."

"Because you had what I heard Grand'mere tell Denise was a 'trying experience'? Because that man chased you?"

"Yes, I suppose so," Elizabeth agreed, surprised that Theresa knew of it, not caring for the avid look in her eyes.

"Were you frightened?"

Instead of answering that eager question Elizabeth asked, "Does Denise know where you are?"

Theresa made a face. "She is asleep with her hair up in pieces of stocking to curl it, and goose grease smeared all over her face. She will give some man an unpleasant surprise, if she ever marries."

"You have given her the slip again?"

"The door doesn't always lock, especially from the ou
side. Denise gets in a hurry sometimes. I hate being locke
in. I always try the door, just in case. I was never locke
in, before you came."

"You mean before the night in the library?" Elizabet
was encouraged to ask the question by Theresa's calı
manner.

"Yes. I wasn't always allowed to eat with the family o
go into town, but I wasn't treated like a—criminal." Sh
dropped her head, staring at the floor, and then looked u
again from under her brows.

"Bernard said I should apologize for that night in the lı
brary. He said what I did was—was unforgivable, but
don't see why. Everybody loses their temper sometimes
and they don't get locked away."

"It depends on what you do when you lose you
temper," Elizabeth said gently.

It was as if Theresa had not heard her. "Nobody threat
ens them or tells them they will have to go away to th
ward for the insane in the Charity Hospital in New Or
leans. Nobody tells them they are mad, or treats them lik
an animal. They might not treat me like that either if yo
would go away."

"I can't do that." Elizabeth tried to match Theresa'
simple, matter of fact tone so that she would be sure t
understand. "I can't because I have no place else to go."

"You're just saying that. Go back where you cam
from. We were all right before. Bernard will help you. H
wants you to go, too."

"I can't. My home doesn't belong to me anymore. An
I have no money."

"You can find another home. Darcourt will give yo
money. He gets some, sometimes. I can ask him."

"Theresa, Theresa—" The sound of the girl's voice, s
reasonable, so determined, touched a chord of response
Elizabeth wanted to reassure her but did not know how
"It isn't my fault, really it isn't. I never said a word abou
putting you in an insane hospital. Why, I never knew there
was anything wrong with you."

She stamped her foot. "Don't be silly. Anybody can see

132

here is something wrong when a seventeen-year-old girl is kept in short skirts!"

"Seventeen!"

It could be true, the girl was as tall as Elizabeth, and here had been her wiry strength that night they struggled over the lamp.

"You know, and you were scared of me, so you decided o get rid of me just as we knew you would!"

We? Theresa had used that word before.

"No, Theresa, I promise you it isn't true."

"Lies. Nothing but lies! Everybody lies to me!" Her voice was rising and rage invading the rational look of her eyes. She began to advance on Elizabeth.

"Theresa!"

The harsh voice of the Frenchwoman halted the girl. The blue moire taffeta of her dressing gown seemed frivolous compared to the black she usually wore. As she walked into the room with quick, angry steps the ruchings that swept the floor about her feet made a whispering sound. The small hoops swinging in her ears caught the light with a sheen that was echoed by the goose grease on her face. Over the knots of rolled hair studding her head she had donned a wrinkled muslin mob cap.

Theresa spun around, all expression draining from her face until she looked plain and dull-witted. Her mouth fell open but she seemed bereft of speech.

"I don't know how you did it, my girl, but this will be the last time you get away from me. I am having bolts installed the first thing in the morning! Then we shall see how much wandering you do."

"Denise—you wouldn't—"

"See if I don't. I am tired of receiving complaints of incompetence and being questioned as if my word was good or nothing. What they expect of me I don't know, I am no gaoler. *Mon Dieu!* You would try the patience of a saint. I don't know whether you are an imbecile or a demon. *Non,* here shall be no more complaints when I have you safe behind a bolted door!"

"I will go to Bernard," Theresa said in a low voice. "I will tell him how I am treated and ask him to free me. He will not be pleased at your treatment of me."

"By all means. Go to your step-brother, if you think he will believe you before me, after the things you have done. You should have thought of the consequences before you went off on a mad tear." A shade of triumph lit Denise' narrow face. She was enjoying taking her spite out on the girl.

Theresa clenched her hands into fists. "You are a witch and I hate you, a beastly, ugly witch, and that is all you will ever be. No matter how much you simper in front of a mirror or make calf eyes at him, my brother will never look at you. Darcourt has more taste."

Denise's hand flashed out as she slapped Theresa in the face. "Impertinent little wretch. You will be sorry you spoke to me like that."

"Denise!" Elizabeth could not help the exclamation. "Surely there was no need for that."

The Frenchwoman's black eyes glared at her with a maniacal anger. Spots of color flamed on her cheeks. "You know nothing of the circumstances. It is not for you to say what is necessary. It is my thankless task to control this mad creature, not yours."

"That will do, Denise."

The quiet masculine tone stopped the tirade short. Bernard stood just inside the room. In his hand he carried a book, his forefinger still marking his page. He wore a dressing gown over his evening clothes. Beneath its large rolled collar his white silk evening shirt could be seen, though he wore no coat or cravat.

"We will not need you any longer. Take Theresa to her room at once, and keep her there. I will speak to you later." His voice was quiet but he emphasized the last words with such clarity that Denise blanched.

Gripping the arm of the crying girl, Denise pulled her from the room.

When the sound of their footsteps had faded down the hall, Bernard still stood regarding Elizabeth with a thoughtful expression. Elizabeth fidgeted under this steady gaze, nervously aware of her bare feet showing beneath the hem of her gown. The gown itself was the serviceable type without lace or embroidery, thick, warm, and com-

134

pletely enveloping, but it was still improper for him to see her in it. She would have been more embarrassed if she had felt that he was equally aware of the impropriety. As it was she doubted he really saw her at all.

Trying to move unselfconsciously, Elizabeth reached for the dressing gown that lay across the foot of the bed. She swung it around her shoulders and pushed her arms into the sleeves. When she had jerked the belt tight she felt much better, as if she were armed, though against what she could not say.

As she glanced up at Bernard she caught a glimpse of sardonic humor just fading from his face. Her head came up instinctively and the green of her eyes deepened to the cold dark jade of a winter sea. The candle glow behind her framed her head in a nimbus of fiery light, sending gleams sliding along individual russet strands of her long hair.

"Well?" she said, her uneasiness made a challenge of the word.

Interest flickered in his eyes, an interest coupled with an unwilling appreciation.

"It was good of you to champion Theresa," he said abruptly.

"Good?" She was wary of the compliment.

"After her tantrum in the library the other night."

"Oh." She was surprised at the flat sound of her voice. It was not as if she wanted there to be anything personal in his comment, was it? She went on impulsively, "I'm glad you did not think I was responsible for what happened that night."

"Responsible?"

"Because of what Theresa said."

"That. No, I am familiar enough with her temperament to realize that you were probably not to blame. Usually it takes something upsetting to trigger a violent reaction. Was anything said, that you can remember, that might have set her off?"

Elizabeth felt the warmth of a flush rise to her cheeks as she remembered what had led to her argument with Theresa. Hopefully the dimness of the room would hide it from Bernard. She wished she had never brought up the

135

subject. Still, she could answer with a negative truthfully enough: it had not been anything she had said to Theresa that had set her off.

"Are you certain?"

"Yes, of course." she answered steadily.

Bernard ran his fingers through his hair, ruffling the smoothness. "I don't know. I would have sworn she would never have turned violent. She isn't mad, just backward. She is like a child, a temperamental ten year old."

"She told me she was seventeen," Elizabeth said, speaking quietly, afraid Bernard would stop, that he would think better of this impulse to explain to her.

"She is, physically, but her mind is the mind of a child much younger. She has never grown up. It is as if she stopped growing three years ago and reverted to childhood."

That would explain the short dresses, the hair worn down when most young ladies put theirs up at the age of fifteen or sixteen. But it did not explain the rages, the attempts to harm her. Bernard must have seen the doubt in her face, for he went on.

"In most ways. Theresa is normal, childish certainly, but a normal child. But lately she has developed an uncontrollable temper. She can not bear to be denied anything. It has been worse since you came. I would have sworn that in spite of her rages she would never hurt a fly, until you came. She was never sensitive to her condition or defensive of it. She was truly like a child, she played with toys, was happiest with some simple game. Now it is almost as though she were trying to grow up emotionally, or was being forced to do so."

His eyes came to rest on Elizabeth's face again, as if despite her protests, Elizabeth thought uncomfortably, he suspected she might have had something to do with it. Was it possible? Could Theresa, in her sensitive mental state, detect the falseness of her position? It did not seem reasonable that she could.

"Why is Theresa like she is? What happened?"

Now Bernard became evasive. "Who can tell? God's will, perhaps."

He turned toward the door. Elizabeth followed him to

see him out and close the door behind him, more a courtesy than a necessity.

Just as she began to close the heavy door, Bernard swung back, one hand going out to stop it. "You seem to be recovering from your—accident."

"Yes. I'm feeling much better," she answered carefully. "There was no need to treat me like an invalid."

"I was under the impression that women enjoy playing the invalid." His smile was bleak.

"Some do, and some don't."

He reached out and took her hand, which had been resting on the door jamb. Turning it over he examined the deep scratch that slashed across the palm.

"The overseer that I dismissed has not been found," he said frowning, running his thumb over the callouses at the base of her fingers, gently outlining the scratch. "He has left the parish, apparently, possibly the state. We could find no evidence that he was ever on the plantation, or, as far as that goes, that anyone else was. The thick grass and leaves cushioned what footprints there might have been. Regardless, you need not be frightened. Nothing of the kind will happen again." His voice hardened. "This is a promise."

Quickly he carried her hand to his mouth. His lips brushed near the raw scratch with a feather kiss, and then he was gone.

In spite of Bernard's assurances it was a long time before she slept. She longed to feel reassured, to know again that nearly forgotten state of security, but too many things prevented it. Not the least of which was a haunting suspicion that she had been taken in by Bernard's concerned manner, lulled into trusting him by some emotion that would not bear daylight.

CHAPTER 9

"Bernard told me about Theresa," Elizabeth told Grand'mere next morning. They were having coffee and croissants on the upper gallery. They sat in the shade, but the sunlight inched toward them across the floor as the morning advanced.

"Did he? I am glad. I have been encouraging him to do so. It was not fair to allow you to remain in ignorance."

"It is sad. I would hate something like that to happen to a child of mine."

"It has been a great shock and a disappointment, this latent streak of violence in her. She was such a sweet child, very seldom into trouble, and then usually because she was following someone else. She was always easily led. Oh, she was mischievous, all children are, but I never expected her to turn out this way."

"You think then that she is responsible for the things that have happened?" She waited tensely for the answer.

Grand'mere pushed her steel spectacles up from where they had slid down her nose. When she spoke her voice had a flat sound.

"She must be."

"Last night—and also that night in the library—she spoke of someone who had told her that I intended to put her away. Perhaps someone else put her up to all these things."

"My dear, who? I know you have had a few distressing experiences, but you must not let such ideas run away with you."

138

"You said yourself that she was easily led—"

"No, no. What sane person would do such things? I prefer to believe Theresa mad than to entertain such a possibility."

But was the older woman's agitation the result of this disturbing idea, or was it that she did not wish Elizabeth to pursue this line of thought? Well, she could not prevent her from doing that. She sat resting her elbows on the arms of her chair, clasping her cup in both hands, sipping it without noticing that it had grown cold. Rousing herself at last, she turned to Grand'mere.

"I have been meaning to ask, what has become of the key to my room?"

"Key? Odd that you should ask, Bernard was asking about the keys himself only yesterday. We never lock our rooms, you know, not when it is just the family. The outside doors are locked after the servants retire to their quarters in the back at night. I had to refer Bernard to Denise. And of course you must see her too, though I cannot blame you for wanting to lock yourself in. Denise has kept the keys for me for some years now. I gave up all pretense of being the chatelaine—that was synonymous with being the keeper of the keys in the old days. It was much too fatiguing. Which reminds me. I must ask her if she removed the chapel key from my reticule. It is gone, but I don't remember giving it to her. But perhaps I did, I'm becoming forgetful these days."

Elizabeth smiled in commiseration. She wondered whether the antagonistic Frenchwoman would release her bedroom key even if she could find a convenient time to ask for it.

Grand'mere crumbled a croissant and threw the pieces at a green chameleon streaking across the floor.

"There is something else," she said broodingly. "I have been sitting here debating whether I should tell you. Theresa was here at the house the day Gaspard died. It was being built then, you remember. Gaspard had brought her with him in the carriage. For a step-father and step-daughter they were close, and Gaspard was indulgent with her. The carpenters had gone; it was getting late. My son had climbed up to inspect the framework, the ceiling joists or some such thing; a foolhardy thing to do. A storm was coming up with thunder and lightning. He fell and broke his neck. Theresa was a perfectly normal child until that day. She has not been the same since. Rainstorms, thunder and lightning, have always affected her badly."

"Because she saw him die?"

"We hope that is all."

"You mean you, and Bernard, believe she might have been in some way responsible?"

"I'm not sure what Bernard thinks. Like Gaspard, he has always been indulgent with her. He has a quieting effect upon her when she has one of her tantrums. I confess it is hard to see how a young girl could have caused my son's death, and yet I, at least, cannot overlook the possibility."

As she finished speaking she glanced back over her shoulder. Loud voices raised in argument could be heard from inside the house. Exasperation crossed the old lady's face but her depression seemed to lift as if she welcomed the change in the trend of her thoughts.

"That woman! She has not a particle of sense when it comes to handling Darcourt. To think my son rescued her from the eternal mourning of widowhood so that his two sons could have the warmth of a mother's love. Bah! Ridiculous ninny! And stupid to boot. Anyone who would use a deadly poison like arsenic to give herself a fashionably wan complexion is an imbecile. Not that she doesn't need something to overcome a tendency toward floridness caused by overeating, a fondness for wine, and tight lacing. It was a mistake to leave Darcourt's allowance in her hands, almost as bad as leaving him without a part of the estate. It would have been much better to leave the allowance to Bernard. He could have been a steadying influence. As it is Alma always makes a terrible scene, but then invariably she gives Darcourt what he wants."

A door slammed inside and footsteps came their way.

"Would you care for a cup of coffee, my boy?" Grand'mere asked as Darcourt strode out onto the gallery.

He shook his head and went to sit on the balustrade with a frown knitting his brows as he stared out over the lawn.

"Positive?" She held the pot poised over an extra cup.

Darcourt looked at them sitting at the table as if seeing them for the first time. "Oh. Yes."

"You're very glum," Grand'mere commented as she poured. He smiled as he took his cup from her and blew on the coffee to cool it. "Just thinking."

"Marvelous." Irritation made her voice dry.

A faint color appeared under his skin, but Darcourt unbent. "I was thinking of Theresa. Someone or something has convinced Mother that she is a dangerous lunatic. She is actually afraid of her own daughter. Even Bernard seems to think that she managed to elude Denise long enough to attack Ellen night before last. I can't believe it."

"I'm sure that is understandable. You are her brother."

"Even if I was not I would not believe it. We were children together. Brothers and sisters usually know one another better than anyone else, even their parents. Theresa was never vicious. She would never hurt anything, never. It bothers me to have everyone thinking that she could."

"It is a fact that Theresa attacked Ellen in the library not so long ago."

"Yes, we found them fighting. But was that all there was to it?"

Elizabeth would have liked to know what Darcourt had in mind, but she was too much aware of her own part in the struggle in the library to ask. He did not seem to be directly accusing her of anything, however. She kept her eyes on her sèvres china cup, running a finger along the gold band of its rim and over the smooth, apricot-colored sides.

"Darcourt! I want to talk to you."

Alma Delacroix sailed out onto the gallery. Then she checked herself when she saw the table in the corner with Grand'mere and Elizabeth seated at it. Her eyes were black in the dead white of her liberally maquillaged face. Above them her black brows lifted and her nostrils were flared as she tried to recover her poise and disguise her temper.

"Maman?" Darcourt said, his eyes gleaming with amusement at her predicament.

Finally Alma smiled. "I would like a word with you, *mon fils*," she said in a coaxing voice.

"By all means." He did not move.

"Alone."

A brooding look closed over his face and his gold-flecked brown eyes narrowed. Still he did not move.

"Must I remind you—"

"Ah no, Maman," he interrupted. "I know who holds the purse strings."

"You are being insolent!"

"Doubtless."

"I cannot and will not abide it." When Darcourt sat on unmoving her voice dropped to a chiding, sorrowful note and she moved to his side. "Come, my son. Let us not quarrel."

Grand'mere, from the look on her face unable to abide the scene any longer, rose abruptly. The action shook the small table and the silver coffeepot teetered on its slender legs. Alma swooped with startling agility for such a large woman, and put a stilling hand on the ornate lid just as Elizabeth, sitting beside it, touched it.

"Thank you, you were both very quick," Grand'mere said before she walked away with slow dignity. In a moment they could hear her giving orders in the hall to have the breakfast dishes cleared away.

"Now what ailed her?" Darcourt asked.

"Old age," Alma answered viciously.

"Don't depend on it." A look Elizabeth could not understand passed between Darcourt and his mother.

"I will leave you also, if you will excuse me," she said, rising to her feet. Neither Darcourt nor his mother answered her, probably because they were too intent on themselves. But as she walked away she could feel them staring after her. As soon as she was out of their sight, she heard Alma's haranguing voice begin.

Despite the bright sunlight outside, the hall was dim. The wide windows at the far end beckoned, and having nothing else to do she walked toward them and stood looking out.

There was no gallery at the back of the house. The win-

142

dows looked down on the garden with larkspur and daisies and early roses in full bloom. Beyond the garden the ground sloped to the bayou, its banks overgrown with wild azalea and willows genuflecting to their reflections in the water. Elizabeth did not see the beauty. She was thinking of Theresa.

Apparently the girl had never said why she had attacked Elizabeth, had never mentioned that she had seen Elizabeth going through Bernard's desk. Did she remember? Or did she think no one would believe her? Whatever the reason, in some strange manner the fact made Elizabeth feel guilty, as if she had taken advantage of Theresa's weakness. And hadn't she? Since Theresa's visit to her room the night before she had stayed in Elizabeth's mind, with her shadowed eyes, her pathetic dignity. She could not shake the idea that she was in part responsible for Theresa's disturbance and her confinement. She could not help thinking that Theresa would have been better if she had never come.

Deep inside her chest ironic laughter bubbled. *If she had never come* . . . she wished she had never come, not in deceit, not as Ellen, Joseph's mother. The weight of her deception grew daily heavier. At times she felt an almost unbearable compulsion to confess, to tell them who she really was. Added to her old fear that they would guess she was a fraud was a new one: that one day she would blurt out the truth. It was funny.

Fleetingly she thought back to the day in the woods when Bernard had come upon her under the dogwood tree and told her that he was Joseph's legal guardian. That feeling of being in a trap she had experienced had increased a dozen times over, and so had that impression that there was a certain justice in what was happening to her. She could not escape the knowledge that she had no one to blame but herself.

After a while she heard Darcourt and his mother come into the hall from the front gallery. Alma went to her room and Darcourt continued on to descend the stairs. Elizabeth half turned toward them, but they did not seem to notice her there at the end of the hall. When Darcourt's footsteps had ceased and the front door slammed behind

143

him, Elizabeth walked down the hall toward her own room, wondering what she could do with herself. Grand'mere had given her a piece of embroidery to do to pass the long, idle hours, but the prospect of returning to it did not have much appeal.

The two doors nearest her on the left were open. One was to the schoolroom, which had beyond it the small bedroom that had been allocated to Denise. Connected to the schoolroom by a common door was the old nursery where Theresa slept. As she passed the second of the doors Elizabeth heard a small sound. She stopped, listening, but she did not have to hear it clearly to know what it was.

It was Theresa. She was crying.

Elizabeth stood immobile, listening. Two maids in blue dresses, white aprons and white tignons, mounted the stairs and looked back at her curiously before going on out to clear the table on the gallery. Behind them came a small Negro errand boy of about ten who eyed her out of the corners of enormous eyes before he took his seat on the long hall bench and tucked his bare feet under it. He had taken a piece of grubby string from his pocket and begun to play cat's cradle before Elizabeth moved on down the hall past him.

Callie, as watchful as a setting hen, looked up at Elizabeth as she opened the door. She had pulled her chair to the window for light while she hemmed a new supply of diapers for Joseph. The baby lay on the floor picking at one of the pieced squares of the quilt that served him as a pallet.

He had squirmed and turned so that his long white dress was twisted under him. Elizabeth knelt beside him and straightened it out, pulling it down over his feet and spreading it out like a fan, tickling him a little, rolling him back and forth in play. He laughed and reached for her with his closed hands, wanting to be picked up. Her heart contracted with the pain of love and fear, the fear that harm might come to him. She picked him up, hugging him to her.

Still, she could not get the sound of Theresa's crying out of her head. She remembered that first day at Oak Shade when she had surprised Theresa outside her room. The

144

girl had asked about the baby then. What was it she had said? *"It might die, babies do, sometimes."* Yet, she had been happy when Elizabeth had asked her if she would like to see Joseph. Bernard had appeared then and she had not come in. Theresa had never seen him.

Unless it was when she carried him to the head of the stairs and left him.

A chill ran along her nerves at the thought, and her half-formed impulse to take Joseph to see Theresa suffered a check. It seemed mad, a crazy thing to do, a terrible risk, also. But in some intuitive manner she knew it was right. Before she could change her mind she stood up with the baby in her arms and started toward the door.

"I'll be back in a little while," she said in answer to Callie's questioning expression.

She knocked firmly on the door of Theresa's room. She heard approaching footsteps, and then Denise stood in the half-open door.

"What is it?" the Frenchwoman asked. Her voice contained the slight note of insolence that she always used when speaking to Elizabeth alone.

"I would like to see Theresa," Elizabeth replied evenly.

"I cannot allow that."

"Oh? Have you been ordered to keep out all visitors?"

Denise shrugged, and moved back to let Elizabeth enter. Theresa was sitting on the bed.

"Theresa?" Elizabeth came into the room.

Theresa did not answer, but there was a flicker of interest in her tear-drowned eyes.

"You came to see me last night, so Joseph and I have come to see you today."

Theresa sat up. "Joseph, the baby?"

"Yes, of course." Elizabeth tried to smile as if it was the most natural thing in the world. She stepped forward and put the baby on the bed beside Theresa. Joseph protested at being put down, and an anxious look crossed Theresa's face, but though it was difficult, Elizabeth turned her back on him and went to the window.

She threw back the drapes, letting light flood into the room. Dust flew into the air, motes of it turning slowly in the bright sunlight and settled slowly onto the thick scum

145

already on the furniture. Theresa blinked like an owl in the sudden light and drew back, putting up a hand to shield her eyes.

"Come," Elizabeth said, holding out her hand after she had picked up Joseph. "We will go into the schoolroom where it is more pleasant."

Theresa blinked rapidly, staring at the hand Elizabeth offered.

"Don't you want to play with Joseph?"

"He—he will cry." Her eyes were on Joseph, who had stopped fretting the moment Elizabeth picked him up.

"No he won't. I'll show you how to hold him."

"Truly? You will let me hold him?"

"I promise."

To Elizabeth's dismay, tears welled again into Theresa's eyes, but she placed her thin, wiry hand into Elizabeth's and slid down from the four-poster bed.

Denise stood back from the door, watching, a grim expression about her mouth.

Elizabeth looked at her, her green eyes cold. "We will use the schoolroom for now. Will you please see that Theresa's room is thoroughly cleaned? Thoroughly. Change the bed linen. Sweep the rug, dust the furniture, the drapes, the window sills, the bed hangings. Everything. Then have them prepare a bath."

Denise did not move. Her heavy dark brows met over her nose as she frowned.

"You do not have to do my bidding, that is true," Elizabeth said slowly, "but you would be well advised to do it. I am persuaded that Grand'mere would not be pleased with the state of this room, even if it is a prison."

"You have taken so much on yourself, why, I see no reason that you cannot take the ordering of the room upon yourself also," Denise said jerkily.

"I am not responsible. You are." Elizabeth walked to the door and opened it. Then she stood waiting.

Denise wanted to refuse. The struggle moved across her face, pride vying with caution, as she tried to decide if Elizabeth had more influence with Grand'mere than she. Caution won, but the malevolent look she threw at Eliza-

eth before she went out the door was that much more in-
ense because of the defeat of her pride.

The time passed quickly. Toward the end of the visit
Theresa was persuaded to hold Joseph in her arms. She
tared down at the baby and slowly, carefully, she smiled.
t was the first genuine smile Elizabeth had seen on her
ps in a long time.

Theresa examined the baby's fingers, toes, and ears,
narveling at his fingernails, and eyelashes like a new moth-
r. Once she looked up at Elizabeth and opened her
nouth as if to say something, but then she shut her lips
ightly and dropped her head.

When finally Elizabeth left with Joseph in her arms, she
vas thoughtful. Leaving Joseph in Callie's care, she went
1 search of Bernard. She was not sure what she would say
o him, for surely he knew best what was necessary for safe-
uarding Theresa both from herself and others, but she
vanted somehow to help the girl. She was certain Denise
vas not the best gaoler, as resentful as she was of the po-
ition. Even if it was true, as they seemed to believe, that
Theresa was responsible for the things that had happened,
ad done them during some childish fit of temper, she did
iot deserve to be punished. It was not her fault precisely,
ot if she was mentally disturbed. Elizabeth could not
dmit even to herself that she was finding the idea ques-
ionable.

Bernard was not in the house, she learned from Sam-
on. She should have known he was not likely to be in at
his hour of the morning. He was not a gentleman of lei-
ure, since he preferred to keep a personal eye on his
roperty.

Wandering into the library, she looked at the titles in-
cribed in gold leaf on the leather-bound books. She was
ot particularly interested in reading, however, and none
f them looked engrossing enough to take her mind from
er problems. The humidor that Theresa had thrown at
er that night had been returned to its place on the table.
Elizabeth lifted the lid to sniff the fragrance of Louisiana
'erique mixed with mild Virginia tobacco, and then re-
laced it. She touched the whale oil lamp sitting on the

147

desk, straightened the blotter and pewter ink well, and a
justed the sandlewood box holding cigars. Swinging res
lessly away she noticed the cuspidor beside the fireplace.
was brightly polished and perfectly clean. Grand'mere w
so vociferously against chewing tobacco that neither Be
nard nor Darcourt used it. According to Darcourt, few
their friends dared to do so in Grand'mere's presence. Sl
was capable of upbraiding them about that disgustir
habit, one that she pronounced as unfit for gentleme
though most gentlemen were guilty of it these days. Smol
ing, whether pipe or cigar, was limited to this room an
the galleries. Grand'mere was likely to cough dramatical!
and sniff the drapes for the odor at the least whiff
smoke in the rest of the house.

Smiling a little, Elizabeth walked to the windows. Tl
sun high overhead had gone behind a strip of clouds, din
ming the room. It would soon be midday. Surely Be
nard would return for the noon meal. He usually di
While she was here she should thank him for coming
her rescue. She never had. She hated to broach the sul
ject, however; it gave her an unpleasant feeling in the p
of her stomach. The confusion of doubts and suspicior
that she had shoved to the back of her mind made he
want to forget the incident.

Fingering the lace panels at the windows, she stared ur
seeingly over the lawn. She felt a sense of indebtedness to
ward Bernard. Whatever his reasons, he had pulled he
from among the thorns that night. Once or twice, she ha
felt the impulse to give him her permission to use th
money that he had wanted, a gesture of gratitude, she suf
posed. An empty gesture, perhaps, from his point of view
since he had told her he did not really need her permit
sion. Still, it was an admission that she had been spiteful i
withholding it in the first place. That should mean som
thing to him.

Last night he had kissed her hand. Slowly she close
her fingers over the scratches on the palm where his lif
had touched. He had kissed her hand before, a casual sa
lute identical to that he would offer any other marrie
woman. A gentleman did not kiss the hands of unmarrie

adies, at least, not in public. But had that salute been different, or was it her imagination? Did she want it to be different?

The thought shocked her, yet how else could she explain her behavior? By coming here to this room, with the intention of interceding in Theresa's behalf and actually thinking the man who might have been the one who attacked her—and by thinking of offering him the use of the money Felix had left Ellen—she was going against her own best interests. Was her desire to remain at Oak Shade so strong that she was willing to placate those who had tried to harm her and sacrifice the welfare of Joseph and Callie?

She could not do that. What was she thinking of, to have come so far toward that betrayal? She could not in any way afford to be that trusting.

Footsteps coming toward the door made her turn. So confused were her thoughts that she ran her eyes around the room looking for a place to conceal herself, feeling completely unable to explain what she was doing waiting here. She was afraid that in her state, if she were forced to try to explain her presence she would say the wrong thing. Then, taking a deep breath, she stood still. An appearance of dignity must be preserved at all costs. She must not appear flustered. She composed her face.

The door opened. Darcourt sauntered in and Samson closed the door soundlessly behind him.

"So here is where you got off to. Grand'mere was wondering." Stopping at the desk he lifted the lid on the sandalwood box, took a cigar, and let it close with a snap. He asked her permission to smoke, and when she gave it he reached into the holder on the desk and took out a handful of matches.

Seeing her gaze, he said, "Oh, I never take just one. The things aren't all that trustworthy, you know. Just as likely to fizzle out on you as not. Better than the old flint and tinder contraptions, though."

Grateful for the small talk to cover her tension, Elizabeth answered with a smile. "I think so too, but Grand'mere will give you a different opinion."

Darcourt laughed. "The devil's work. She doesn't trust them. Natural, I guess, for the old not to trust new things. Come to think of it, she doesn't trust much of anything."

"A wise old lady."

"Oh, come now. Cynicism is unbecoming at your age. Wait for your gray hairs."

"Does age have anything to do with it?"

He spread his hands in mock ignorance. "You ask me, a golden-haired child?"

"You are very bright, after your gloom this morning," Elizabeth said. Then she regretted her impulsive words since they might remind Darcourt of the unpleasantness with his mother that she and Grand'mere had witnessed. She need not have worried.

"It doesn't take much to put the sun back into my sky." His grin was wide, filled with a bubbling merriment.

"Have you heard of a new thoroughbred to back them or found a twenty-dollar gold piece?"

Realizing suddenly that he could not sit as long as she stood, she walked to the couch and sank into it, glancing up at him quizzingly.

"Nothing so frivolous."

"Oh?"

He lowered his voice to a near whisper, though the smile never left his eyes. "I've discovered the way to make my fortune. All that the thing needs is a few details."

"Congratulations. Is it a secret?"

"For now, but not for long. I'll take Theresa and my mother away from here, and the rest of the Delacroix can —except for Celestine who will I hope go with me—but I had better wait until it's done before I make plans."

"I imagine so."

"That's what I like about you. No purely idle phrases. Most girls would have said something nonsensical, like 'Oh, it doesn't hurt to dream,' or else assure me that I'll be a great success without knowing the first thing about it. Not you."

"No, I would never say that," Elizabeth replied, staring for a moment over his shoulder.

"I had an idea you were one of the ones who know better."

150

She glanced up quickly, meeting his tawny gold eyes. Then she laughed shortly, not at all sure she liked that impression of herself.

"What would most girls say to that?"

"They would turn coy, I expect, even Celestine. Coyness, evasiveness, either is a good tactic for avoiding unwanted personal comments."

"Even Celestine?"

"You think she would speak her mind?" He shook his head, a bitter twist appearing at the corner of his mouth. "Never. A devious woman, is Celestine. Beautiful, but devious. Also mercenary. She is determined to lead Bernard to the altar, but does she entice him, persuade him with money? Oh yes, but she doesn't depend on it. She holds the whip hand and she knows it. The lash that will finally goad Bernard into matrimony is honor, the Delacroix honor."

"How can she be satisfied with a marriage like that?"

"Satisfied? She will be radiant, and because she is, no doubt eventually Bernard will be well-pleased also."

"You think so?"

"Why wouldn't he be?" He looked down at the tip of the cigar smouldering between his fingers, while with the fingers of the other hand he broke the match he had used, and bent the broken stem into a circle before tossing it into the fireplace. "Why shouldn't he be? As I said, Celestine is a very beautiful woman."

"Yes." Elizabeth thought of Celestine as she had last seen her, dainty, impeccably groomed in orchid taffeta, very pretty even with the sneer on her delicate cameo face.

"You are in love with her, aren't you?" She had thought once that it might have been a game to Darcourt, a flirtation to relieve his boredom.

"To my sorrow."

"Why are you allowing her to marry Bernard then, if you are sure she doesn't love him?"

"Let her? I've done everything in my power to prevent it except—"

"Except?"

"Kill her, or offer her money."

"And so the need for a fortune?"

"And so the need for a fortune," he agreed, nodding slowly.

"Oh, Darcourt, why—?" The question broke from her but she could not finish it for the sudden stillness that came over him and the black look that entered his eyes.

"Who can explain what draws a man to a certain woman? I can't, can you? I wonder at times if Bernard is at all attracted to Celestine, or if he only pretends out of what he conceives to be his duty."

"I—I wouldn't know."

"You might find out," he said, frowning with a speculative look through narrowed lids. "Smile at him instead of frowning all the time. Stop avoiding him."

"Oh, come, why should I do that?"

"To see if he is susceptible to red-haired beauty, of course. You must be aware that you already have a powerful attraction—I'm talking about your widow's portion. When you remarry it will revert to Joseph's estate. That, I expect, was to keep any man from marrying you for your money. Any man except Bernard, that is. Naturally when your money returns to Joseph's estate Bernard will have complete control over it too. Twenty thousand dollars is a powerful incentive just now, you'll agree, with banks closing their doors right and left? Added to your own charms?"

"You must think everyone alive is mercenary if you seriously think that Bernard would desert Celestine to marry me for my widow's portion."

"I did say he might need a little encouraging," he reminded her, smiling.

"Oh!" Relief flooded over her. "I thought you were in earnest."

"I was, never more so. Honor or money, a dark beauty or a red-haired one? Which will he choose?"

"Don't be ridiculous," she snapped, her brows drawn together.

"You will never know until you try."

"I don't intend to do any such thing."

He shrugged. "You're probably right not to. On second thought, I doubt Bernard would try to shorten your long mourning for Felix, or, to give him his due, expect you to believe in a sudden overwhelming passion for you. He isn't stupid. It would be more in his style to try to soften your resolve so that you would relinquish the money of your own accord."

"Probably," Elizabeth answered dryly. She did not think Bernard had been trying to influence her in that manner, but now the seeds of doubt were sown. Yet she knew, though apparently Darcourt did not, that there was no need for Bernard to use subterfuge of any kind. He already had the use of her money until such time as she could prove her identity.

"I wonder, how does it happen that you know so much about my affairs?"

"Felix's will was read to all of us, of course, along with the letter from him that told of his marriage and gave his instructions on what to do in the event of his death. A black day, that."

"I see," she said, as she stood up, her lips tightening. "Then everyone knows."

"I'm sorry. I didn't mean to upset you." Darcourt came toward her, a contrite expression on his face. "My fatal tongue. I let it run away with me sometimes."

"No. I'm not upset. It doesn't matter." It was a lie. She knew it, though she tried to convince herself that it was not. Darcourt suddenly left the room. She moved toward the door.

As she neared it the door swung open and Bernard stepped into the room. A smile of surprise crossed his face as he stood with his hand on the knob, blocking her way.

His unexpected appearance held her motionless too long. She felt that she had to say something.

"Theresa," she said, swallowing hard, thankful for the memory. "I wanted to speak to you about her. I don't think it is good for her to be cooped up with only Denise for company. She should have the acquaintance of young people, normal people. It can't be good for her to dress her like a child when she realizes her age and the manner in which she should be dressed."

His dark brows rose. "You are an unlikely supplicant on Theresa's behalf. Why the sudden interest?"

"I—I don't know. I feel sorry for her, I suppose."

"After what she has done to you?"

Elizabeth made a slight negative motion with her head, unable to summon the strength to go into involved explanations without incriminating herself.

"I think you may leave it to me to judge what is best for Theresa. You, after all, have known her for only a short time."

Elizabeth stared at her hands. "That is true. And yet, I wonder if I don't see her more clearly for being a stranger. I can hardly believe—"

"Leave it to me," Bernard repeated when she faltered.

Elizabeth did not answer or try to complete what she had started to say. In truth, she was glad that he had interrupted her, for she did not want to finish the thought.

When she did not go on an oddly intent look came into his eyes. "Was there anything else?"

For a moment she had forgotten what Darcourt had said. Then she remembered.

"No," she said in a hard voice, looking straight into his eyes. "There was nothing else."

She started past him, but he reached out and caught her arm. "Is anything wrong?"

"Of course not," she said, forcing a brittle smile, swallowing on the tears crowding in a hard knot at the back of her throat.

"I don't think you are telling the truth."

Elizabeth thought something like real concern flickered in his black eyes. She was trying to form a rational reply when Celestine spoke from the foot of the stairs.

"No, she is not telling the truth! You may be sure of that!" She let the echoes of her voice fall around her before she went on in a voice that was nearly a whisper.

"But what can you expect from an imposter?"

CHAPTER 10

Elizabeth stood frozen, with the color slowly draining from her face. Bernard's grip on her arm tightened. Together they turned to watch Celestine come down the hall, dragging Callie with her by the arm. Tears poured down Callie's face and a sob tore at her throat as she stumbled toward Elizabeth with her eyes fixed on her face.

Breaking away from Celestine's hold on her, she fell to the floor and clasped her arms around Elizabeth's knees.

"Oh, Mis' Elizabeth! That Mis' Alma told Mis' Celestine everything. Mis' Celestine and her came to your room and they been slapping me and pinching me. Mis' Celestine say she'll have me whipped if I don't tell her everything. She say she'll have Mr. Bernard sell me off the next coffle that comes along and I'll never see little Joseph again. Don't let her! Don't let her do that to me! You won't, will you?"

"No, no. Hush now. It's all right. You couldn't help it. Go back to Joseph now. I hear him crying."

"But—but I got to tell you—"

"It will be all right. I understand, and it's all right. Go back to Joseph," Elizabeth said again quietly, as she helped Callie to her feet. The masquerade was over. Now the calm of despair settled over her, numbing her so that she was surprised to find her hands trembling. She clasped them together at her waist as she watched Callie begin to climb the stairs with a heavy tread, pulling herself up by

155

the bannister and wiping the tears from her face with her white apron.

Celestine did not wait until Callie was out of sight. "This woman was never married to Felix. She is Elizabeth Brewster, the sister of the girl who was his wife. She is without doubt an adventuress of the most flagrant—"

"We will not discuss it in the hallway," Bernard broke into the tirade. "Come into the library."

Celestine stopped short, her mouth open, but she shut her lips and swished past Bernard into the room, holding her skirts away from contact with Elizabeth. Angry color rode high on her cheekbones at Bernard's rebuke, but triumph blazed from under her lowered lashes.

When the door was closed Bernard took his place behind the desk while Darcourt and Celestine seated themselves on the sofa. But Elizabeth was left standing like a criminal before the bench, in negation of the gentleman's code, which did not allow a man to be seated as long as a lady was standing. There was a grim humor for her in the thought. For all purposes she had ceased to be a lady. She could not expect the protection of the code.

Clasping her hands together tighter, she raised her head in a gesture of unconscious pride. She must look composed, she told herself. She must not show fear. And she would not, no matter what happened, beg them to let her stay.

Bernard leaned back in his chair, picking up the miniature sword, with its blade chased in gold and black, that served as a letter opener. He sat pulling it out of its sheath and pushing it back, staring at the top of his desk. As the moments passed and he still did not speak, Celestine moved restlessly and sat forward, opening her mouth. Bernard shot her a glance that made her subside back into the cushions, and then he sighed and looked up at Elizabeth.

"Is it true?"

"Yes."

"Your sister, Ellen, is Felix's wife?"

"She was. She died when Joseph was born."

"I see. So you took her place. Why?"

Her jaws felt locked with tension, but she gripped her hands together and forced herself to speak.

156

"Ellen had planned to come here at Grand'mere's invitation after her child was born. When she died, Joseph became mine. I took care of him, I loved him. But I could not keep him as he should have been kept. There was no money, and our house, the land, all went for the mortgage. You wanted Joseph, Felix's son. That was plain enough from the invitation issued only after you knew that Ellen was to have a child. I was afraid that you would take him away from me. I could not expect to stay here with him as his mother would have, or to carry him away with me once you had seen him and learned that his mother, as well as his father, was dead."

"My dear girl, of course you could have stayed. Oak Shade is a large house and my grandmother would have welcomed with open arms anyone who brought her great-grandchild to her."

"Possibly. But I didn't know that. I did not feel that I could take the chance."

Celestine spoke up. "How do we know that this baby is Felix's son? It might be any child for all we know."

"The birth was recorded by the priest who baptised him, and I did have a copy of the marriage record of my sister and Felix," Elizabeth said steadily. She looked at Bernard, willing him to believe her. He must, for Joseph's sake.

"Forged records, I imagine. The brat is probably her own." Celestine shivered delicately. "She came here for the money, I have no doubt."

"But I didn't know about the money until I got here!"

"So you say," Celestine sneered, and turned to Bernard. "Suppose Felix had mentioned to her sister that he was going to leave the money? She could have known in that case because her sister could have told her. It makes more sense than this trumped up tale we have heard so far."

"It's not true! Ellen knew nothing of the money. I would to God that she had! She could have had decent food, better care, a doctor. She would still be alive instead of dying in a pool of her own blood bringing another Delacroix into the world!" Elizabeth grated out the last word then turned away sharply to hide the tears that sprang into her eyes.

"A fine exhibition, but it proves nothing," Celestine sniffed.

"Celestine," Bernard said abruptly, "Darcourt will see you to your room."

The other girl rose slowly to her feet. "You cannot do this to me, Bernard. I have a right to be present."

"I am sure we owe you a debt of gratitude for your efforts in this, Celestine, but I would rather speak to—Elizabeth alone."

Although he was sending Celestine away, there was nothing in his even, neutral tone that gave any indication of his feelings.

"But Bernard, I—" Celestine stopped, apparently seeing some change of expression in his eyes. "Very well." She took Darcourt's arm with ill grace.

Darcourt had been very quiet during the proceedings, maintaining a thoughtful silence, Elizabeth felt. As he passed her he caught her eye and gave her a bright smile. Several times since she had been in the house she had enjoyed his casual, almost careless, support. She was glad to see that he did not condemn her now.

The closing of the door was loud in the stillness. The anger that Celestine had aroused dissipated slowly, to be replaced by a growing tension that crept along her nerves like pain. Feeling her nails cutting into the palms of her hands, she forced her fingers to relax, staring at them in concentration. Behind her she heard Bernard leave his chair and walk around the desk.

"Do you really think that this is a surprise to me?"

"Wasn't it?" Elizabeth raised her head a fraction.

"I suspected you from that first day. You were too different from the girl Felix had described in his letters. Since he was marrying a strange woman you can imagine the special attention I paid. I remember wondering why he would be so smitten by a woman much like the fiancée he had left at home patiently awaiting his return. You would think that he would have chosen someone entirely different."

"Ellen was not at all like Celestine."

"No? Fragile and dainty, as 'delicate and pretty as a wild flower,' to quote a line of his extravagances."

158

"My sister was not strong, there was no question of assumed airs of delicacy, as is the fashion now."

"You, on the other hand, are obviously strong—you said you were yourself. Remember?"

"Yes," she admitted. "I remember."

"Strong enough to do quite a bit of hard labor if your hands, and the callouses on them, are anything to go by."

She did not answer, remembering the night he had examined so carefully the palm of her hand before he kissed it.

"Didn't you guess there would be letters, that Felix would write to his family about such an important event?" He leaned against the desk, his arms folded over his chest.

"Ellen and I were much alike," Elizabeth said, throwing him a wry smile over her shoulder as she moved away, "other than our constitutions, of course. There was three years difference in our ages, but our coloring and size was much the same. Then, Felix often styled himself a poor correspondent. It seemed a good risk. In any case I thought none of you could have formed any concrete idea of Ellen from a description you might have read once in a letter written many months before."

"And you thought you could get your hands on any letters that might be lying around if you had to in order to prevent us from refreshing our memories? That was what you were doing here in this room the night Theresa and you were down here, wasn't it?"

"Yes," she answered expressionlessly. There seemed no reason to dissemble any longer.

"I thought as much, which is why I kept my own letters in my room under lock and key. That is, I kept them there until last night."

There was such a strange inflection in his voice that Elizabeth turned to face him. Light from the lamp flickered over the bronze of his face, highlighting its strong planes and igniting sparks in the darkness of his eyes.

"Last night," he went on, "I saw the old callouses on your hands and I knew you could not be Ellen, so fragile and often bedridden. I was not sure who you were, but I thought that given time, you would tell me. I looked into those deep green eyes of yours and I thought I saw—I don't know. I trusted the way you looked at me; steady sure, without evasion. I burned the letters."

In the silence Elizabeth became aware of the ticking of the ormolu clock on the mantle. It seemed to grow louder as she searched for something to say. She licked her dry lips.

"You burned them?"

"Yes." His voice was harsh as he pushed away from the desk and walked toward her. "A quixotic gesture, was not? I wanted to throw them in your face, but I burned them. Men are fools, always looking for the perfect woman. They put women on pedestals and then are surprised when they lose their balance and fall off. But then they pick them up, dust them off, and put them back. Men need an ideal, even if they have to make one for themselves for lack of the real thing."

Elizabeth watched his advance in some trepidation, her mind in confusion as she tried to understand what he was saying.

"I looked at you and I saw your steadfast eyes and I ignored the lies and pretending, and I thought: *There is reason. She will confess it.* I told myself that it was not the money, that eventually you would deny the settlement. But you did not, and now I will never know whether you would have or not."

He put out his hands as if to catch her shoulders; then before they touched her, he let them drop.

The knowledge that he had thought of her as being so much nobler and more truthful than she could ever have dared to be, was like a goad. As she felt the sting, she struck back.

"You don't think that it was a little unfair of you to use persuasion in this purely righteous cause?"

"What do you mean?"

"I mean that you have been more than ordinarily attentive in the past few days. You have tried in every way possible to make me feel the ingratitude of my position and to influence my decision," she accused him bitterly.

His eyes narrowed. "You are wrong. I have not tried every way."

160

She saw his intention flare into his eyes and she took a hasty step backward. "I didn't mean—"

His arm slid around her, gripping her waist, and then she was roughly silenced. His lips were warm, but cruel. He paid no attention to her struggles in the steel circle of his arms. Against her his body was lean and unyielding. It was a deliberate punishment for questioning his integrity, and it was also a punishment for being less than he had expected her to be. After her first panic, Elizabeth realized in shame that he had reason for his action. She herself had disillusioned him and then taunted him with it. She had entered his home under false pretenses, accepted a legacy, in theory at least, that did not belong to her. Regardless of her motives she could not deny her guilt. She ceased to resist him. Slowly, almost imperceptibly, a treacherous tenderness crept into the kiss. Instinctively, like a child who has been hurt, Elizabeth responded to its gentle touch.

Suddenly Bernard thrust her from him. He stared at her, his breathing rough and a grim look about his mouth.

Wave on wave of color burned to Elizabeth's hairline. In the quiet of the room there was a loud rustling as the folds of her skirts settled into place. Tears rose painfully behind her eyes, and she bowed her head.

"Ellen—"

Bernard took a step toward her again, calling her by the name he had come to associate with her in his mind.

"My name is Elizabeth!"

She flung her head up, staring at him with wet, burning eyes, and then she turned and ran toward the door. As her hand touched the knob a knock sounded, and hard on it, the door opened. Just in time, Elizabeth stepped back.

"Dinner is on the table, Mr. Bernard," Samson said. He bowed gravely as he spoke, though he shot Elizabeth a curious look from the corner of his eye as she slipped behind him from the room.

By the time she had closed her own bedroom door behind her, her tears had dried and her resolve was set. She would not stay at Oak Shade another day. She could not. She could not face Celestine's ill-concealed delight at her unmasking or witness Grand'mere's pained surprise. Den-

161

ise, no doubt, would be jubilant, smirking openly, and even the other servants would look at her with sidelong curiosity, entertained by the novelty of it. Theresa, too, would be glad. Not one of them would be sorry to see her go.

"My dear?" Grand'mere called from the other side of the door connecting the rooms. "Aren't you coming down to dinner?"

There was nothing in her voice to tell that she had been informed. What were they waiting for? Perhaps Bernard would tell her at the dinner table.

"I'm not very hungry." Elizabeth called back.

"Don't you feel well?"

"I—not really. Perhaps I am catching a spring cold."

"Can I send you anything? Some cologne for your forehead? A cool drink? Perhaps some orange flower water?"

"No—no, thank you Grand'mere. I will be perfectly fine. I'll just rest."

"Very well."

She heard the old lady walk away. She was, under her acerbity, a person of great kindness and tact. Elizabeth wished it was not necessary for her to learn how she had been duped. Sighing, she turned back to her thoughts.

When she was sure that Grand'mere had gone down to dinner, she began to collect the few things that she would need, the barest necessities, into a bundle. Going into the next room, she gathered together the things Joseph and Callie would need, making another bundle of these. Joseph, asleep in his crib, moved restlessly, but did not awake. Callie had gone down to the kitchen for her dinner. The Negro nurse would have to be told, but not immediately. She might not be able to go quietly through the rest of the afternoon in close association with Grand'mere if she knew of their impending escape, especially not after her ordeal with Celestine.

When the bundles were tied securely, she pushed them under her own bed. Going to the armoire she took down her reticule and counted her money. There was enough for food for a few days and perhaps a week's lodging if they could find a clean, cheap rooming house. There was no

162

oney left over for stagecoach fare. They would have to
ok to heaven for help. The prospect was daunting, but
e did not shrink from it. There was no other way.

She would go south to New Orleans, she thought, sink-
g down on the bed. In a large town it would be easier to
sappear, as well as easier to find some kind of employ-
ent. There were millinery shops and dressmakers, or she
ight even be able to take in laundry if they could find a
rmanent place to stay. She would find something to do
keep Callie and Joseph and herself. She would not let
e Delacroix have him. This house was no place for a
ild to be raised. There was something wrong with the
ry atmosphere. It was full on crosscurrents of malicious
ite and suppressed violence, coupled with a heavy, un-
mfortable feeling of impotence, as if there was nothing
at could be done to remedy the situation that would not
worse than maintaining it.

There was much to think of, much to be done. She
uld attend to it in a moment. She was so tired. The
asquerade had been more of a strain than she had
own. It was true. She was relieved that it was over. She
uld be more relieved when she was far away and could
gin at last to put the last few weeks from her mind. Her
es closed.

The sun had coasted down the sky and the room was in
dow when she awoke. Her mouth was dry, and her
ad ached dully. She felt heavy, weighted down with
ep so deep that it had been like unconsciousness. The
o of a knocking sound lingered in her mind. Then as
sound came again she jolted awake.

"Yes?"

'It is I, Denise. Theresa wishes you to come to her in
schoolroom." The message was given in a voice devoid
expression, but the lack of expression carried its own
ssage of disapproval. Elizabeth tried to detect the
mph she had expected when Denise learned of her real
ntity, but it was not there. Obviously Denise did not
w that she was an imposter. But why not?

'Now?"

"Yes, if you please. Theresa is very anxious for you to come."

"Tell her—tell her I will be there as soon as I can."

"Very good, Madame."

Madame. Then she certainly did not know. It was odd. What reason could Bernard have for keeping the information to himself? Or could it be that the information had not yet filtered down to the servants?

She washed her face and smoothed her hair, and then shook out her dress. It was crumpled, but it did not seem to matter enough to change. Her nap had not refreshed her. Depression clung to her. The heaviness of regret dragged at her mind.

When she was ready to go she put her hand on the doorknob, and then as tiredness swept over her, she leaned her head on the closed door. Why was she doing this? She did not want to go and make conversation with this sullen disturbed girl, someone whom she would never see again after tonight. What would she say to her? What was there to say?

Sympathy. That was the reason. Sympathy because she knew how Theresa felt. She was caught in a trap of her own making, just as Elizabeth had been. There was nothing that either of them could do or say to undo what had been done.

Why was that so terrible? Why did it matter so much? She knew why with a sudden clarity, but she could not allow herself to think of it, just as she had not allowed herself to dwell on the way Bernard had treated her in the library. Suddenly, as if fleeing from her thoughts, she twisted the knob in her hand and left the room.

Theresa herself opened the door. Her eyes sparkled with excitement as she drew Elizabeth inside. Her hair had been put up in gleaming curls drawn back from a center part, and at her throat she wore a garnet on a fine gold chain that she kept touching as if to see that it was still there.

"Bernard has given this necklace to me. It is a symbol that I have grown up," she said. "It belonged to his mother, and it is very precious to him and shows he trusts me

164

He says that I am to have my skirts let down as soon as it can be managed. Isn't it exciting? I owe it to you for speaking to Bernard for me. I just had to thank you!"

She pirouetted, showing off her hair, gracefully balancing its weight on her slender neck. It was an amazing transformation, though Elizabeth could not help but feel that the happiness of Theresa's smile was more important than the new hair arrangement.

"I don't imagine Bernard has allowed you to have these things on my account," she said easily.

"I don't know of any other reason. Denise said that he mentioned that you had spoken to him, though she was being mean about it when she said it. He has given orders that I am to have more freedom, if I earn it. And I am to be dressed at all times as befits my age, and treated in the same way."

"That is wonderful," Elizabeth could not help smiling at the younger girl's transparent joy.

"I only hope the excitement does not make the child ill!" Denise stepped from the bedroom, her back stiff, her manner unrelenting.

"I am not a child, Denise," Theresa said, but some of the animation went out of her face, and it seemed an effort for her to hold on to her pleasure.

"Soon you will be going down to dinner!" Elizabeth spoke gaily, trying to overcome the blight Denise had cast on Theresa's spirits.

"Perhaps I will," she agreed.

"Will what, my sweet?" Darcourt strolled into the room, swinging the door shut behind him.

Theresa ran toward him. "Just look at me, Darcourt! I have my hair up and I'm to have long dresses. Ellen just said that I may soon be having my meals downstairs in the dining room. Aren't you pleased?"

A strange look passed over his face. "You look very pretty, but much too grown up to be my little sister. I'm not sure I didn't like you better the other way." The look he threw Elizabeth held worry, as if he felt the experiment would turn out badly.

"Why did you say that?" Theresa asked, her lips beginning to tremble.

"Don't cry, sweet," Darcourt begged, now contrite. "I didn't mean it. You will have to control your tears better, you know, if you are to go out into society. Of course I like your hair and I am happy for you. It was only a sentimental notion. Forgive me?"

As Theresa smiled up at him he turned toward Denise. "Before I forget, Mother needs you. She is having recourse to the hartshorn and vinegar again. I don't imagine we will see much more of her today."

"Is she ill?" Theresa turned pale.

"Don't worry," he said with a weary cynicism. "She has only been celebrating her victory with too much enthusiasm."

"Victory?"

Consternation flitted over his features, but he was able to reply with creditable casualness, "Heavens, don't ask me. I try not to become involved in all the domestic squabbles and feminine wrangles."

Denise, her face a picture of mystified curiosity, left the room. Theresa stared after her with a dissatisfied look before she turned away with a shrug. She smiled suddenly. "I'm the hostess, aren't I? I wonder if they would bring coffee and cakes and lemonade if I asked for it?"

Darcourt raised his brows at this rather audacious proposal from his retiring sister, but he reassured her. When Theresa had stepped to the door he looked at Elizabeth. "I am sorry about this morning," he said softly, "it must have been an ordeal for you."

"It doesn't matter. It's over now." It did no harm to pretend.

"I wish there was something I could do. I think you would have been good for Oak Shade, and for Joseph."

"Would have been?"

"Bernard cannot let you stay, you know. His pride, the pride of the Delacroix family, will not let him."

"I didn't intend to stay," she said, anger making her careless.

"He will not let you carry the baby with you," he warned. "Not Felix's son. Joseph is a Delacroix and also heir to half this parish."

When Elizabeth did not answer his eyes held steady on

her face, thoughtfulness gathering deep within their gold-flecked depths. "If I can be of any service to you you will let me know, won't you?"

"Why should you want to do that?"

He laughed shortly. "Personal reasons. I know what it is like to look for crumbs beneath the Delacroix table. I know what it is like to want to get away."

He did not elaborate on this cryptic statement and Elizabeth, concentrating on her own problems, did not ask him to explain. She only heard the understanding in his voice.

Theresa turned back into the room. "You should have seen the look on the face of the boy in the hall! He couldn't have been more surprised if one of the family portraits had spoken to him; but he carried my message to the kitchen."

Elizabeth smiled and glanced at Darcourt to see if he was aware of how wonderful it was that Theresa could laugh at herself, but Darcourt was not smiling. There was an intent look in the eyes that followed his sister.

They talked for a few minutes. Theresa was too self-conscious and Elizabeth herself too preoccupied for the conversation to be easy, but it was not as strained as she had feared. Before it had a chance to grow really easy they were interrupted.

Denise flung the door open. She stood in the frame, her hands clasped together and her eyes blazing with satisfaction.

Theresa started to her feet with a cry of surprise. The Frenchwoman ignored her, staring at Elizabeth.

"I knew it! I knew there was something peculiar about you. It was only a matter of time before I found out!"

"What are you talking about?" Theresa stumbled a little as she took a step toward Denise.

"This woman is not who she pretends to be! She is not a widow! She is an impostor! I have it straight from your mother's lips."

Elizabeth got to her feet. She knew there was no way to stop Denise, and so she did not try but stood without speaking, letting the raucous, jeering voice wash over her.

"No," Theresa whispered. "She is my friend."

167

"I could not allow you to be closeted with her another moment. It was my duty to return to you. There is no saying what mischief such a corrupting influence can cause."

"No!"

"But we need not be troubled much longer," Denise went on, ignoring Theresa's outburst. "She will not be staying. I have your mother's assurance that her presence will not be tolerated."

"No! I will—will not—listen! I will not! I will not! I will not!"

Theresa's voice rose to a scream as she raised one hand to her throat as if it hurt her. Feeling the garnet necklace she curled her fingers around it and tore it from her neck. Then in a frenzy she caught at her hair, tearing it free of its pins as sobs shook her and she cried over and over "She was my friend, my friend, my friend—" Like a hurt animal, she bowed over, her arms clasped across her waist, and scuttled toward her room, slamming the door behind her.

Denise turned a pasty white as she saw what she had done.

"Don't stand there, woman," Darcourt snapped. "Get Grand'mere!"

"It's her fault!" Denise screamed, pointing a trembling finger at Elizabeth. "She is the cause of it all, her and her new ideas. Imposter!"

Touched to the quick at last, Elizabeth moved forward to defend herself, but Darcourt turned to her. "Please. Not now. We must quiet Theresa before she hurts herself."

Throwing Elizabeth a baleful glare, Denise hurried away. When she had gone, Darcourt touched Elizabeth's shoulder.

"Perhaps you had better go back to your room. I know you don't want more trouble. I—I'm sorry."

Elizabeth saw that he was right. "Sorry?" she repeated distractedly. "Why should you be sorry?"

"For my mother's part in this."

"Oh. That wasn't your fault." Giving him a tired smile, Elizabeth started toward the door.

Darcourt put out a hand to detain her. "I meant what I

168

aid. If you want help you need only ask. I will be going into town late tonight. If you would like to go with me, wait near the end of the driveway—no, you might be seen. Wait near the chapel."

Elizabeth stared at him a long measuring moment while Theresa's cries came to her through the thick paneling of the door. She had told herself that she must trust to heaven for a way to get away from the house. Here it was. Abruptly she nodded, gave him a brief smile, and left him.

Night was slow in falling. The afterglow lingered in the sky, tinting it shades of rose and lilac and a dusky blue-gray. On the horizon the trees gradually turned from dark green to black, the shadows across the gallery outside the window deepened, and the white cylinders of the columns merged into the darkness. The scent of the flowers, mixed with the smell of roasting meat from the outside kitchen, drifted on the cooling air. A night bird called, a pure and sorrowful note above the song of the crickets.

Elizabeth was left strictly alone. During the long hours she could hear Grand'mere moving about in the other room so that she was prevented from speaking to Callie. Perhaps it was just as well, though being unable to plan on Callie's cooperation increased her apprehension.

For a time she heard voices raised in argument, Darcourt's and his mother's, coming from Alma's room on the other side. She could not make out the words. Later she heard slamming drawers and something scraping across the floor like a trunk. Ordinarily she would have paid no attention, but the movements had a stealthy sound. Thinking of the possible reasons for them and for the quarrel gave her something to occupy her mind.

No one made an attempt to see if she intended to come down to supper. A tray was brought to her room by one of the maids, who placed it on the washstand and went away again without once looking directly at Elizabeth. The story had obviously reached the plantation grapevine.

A short while later she heard Grand'mere leave the room to go down to supper. As soon as the old lady's footsteps were no longer audible she moved swiftly to the door connecting the two rooms and eased it open.

"Callie?"

Without intending it she whispered, and then as she realized what she had done she spoke louder. "Callie?"

"Yes'm?"

Elizabeth walked farther into the room. Grand'mere was indeed out of the room, but even so she hardly dared raise her voice.

"Callie—" she said again, and then took a deep breath. "We are leaving. Tonight."

"What! Mis' Elizabeth, how we going to do that?"

"Not so loud, someone will hear you. Never mind how. I want you to sleep lightly. If Grand'mere does not look sleepy, or if she is slow to go to bed, I want you to encourage her to use her laudanum."

"Yes'm, I—think I can do that."

"Good. Gather together what you want to carry with you, plus a dress to wear. Bring it to my room as soon as you can. When Grand'mere is asleep I want you to get up, wrap Joseph up in his blanket and bring him to my room. You can slip your dress on there. All right?"

Callie nodded, her eyes large but unafraid. She could be trusted.

Returning to her own room, Elizabeth ate her supper slowly to kill time, savoring each bite, each drop of wine, for it might be some time before she was able to eat in peace and comfort again. Even so, there was time and to spare to check the bundles again when Callie brought hers, go over everything to be sure they had what was most needed, and secrete them back under the bed before the maid returned for the tray.

She paced, she tried to read, she stared out the window at the night. At last she heard Grand'mere come up to bed, and then she heard her cross to the door so that she was forewarned when the knock came.

"Elizabeth? Could I speak to you?"

Elizabeth's gaze swept the overhang of the bedspread to see that it concealed the bundles beneath the bed, and then she thought of the dress she was wearing. It was late to be still dressed. Would Grand'mere be suspicious, or would it go unnoticed under the circumstances? Perhaps it would be better to take no chances. In any case she did not feel as though she could bear a lecture just now.

170

"I'm very tired," she called. "Could we postpone it until morning?"

There was no answer for a long moment. "In the morning then," Grand'mere agreed finally, her voice tart, before she went away.

Silently Elizabeth sighed with relief. Then came the longest wait.

At last she heard the creaking of the bed ropes as the old lady in the next room climbed into her four-poster bed. For a little longer there was movement up and down the hall outside, and then the house grew quiet, the last door slammed. The servants left for the night; she could hear them laughing and talking as they made their way to the house servants' quarters directly behind the house. She grew stiff and cold with inactivity. Her nerves stretched as she listened to the creaks and groans of the house settling. A little later the moon rose half-full, as silvery as a scimitar blade, and without comfort in its cold remoteness.

When Callie did not come, Elizabeth began to worry. Perhaps Darcourt would not wait for them. He would think they were not coming. Callie would not be able to take the baby from his bed without waking him and having him cry out. Grand'mere would wake and prevent her from leaving the room. She might even raise the alarm. Then at last there came a brushing sound against the door. When she hurried to open it, Callie stood there with Joseph cradled carefully in her arms. Beyond her Grand'mere lay in her bed in the dark room, the rhythmic breathing of deep sleep whistling softly in and out between her lips.

Elizabeth whispered one word as she held her arms out for the sleeping child. "Hurry."

They crept along the hall and down the stairs, feeling their way in the dark with the help of the pale luminescence of the moon glowing through the windows at the end of the hall. Freezing at each creak of a board, listening for some sound above their own heartbeats thudding in their ears, starting at shadows and praying Joseph would not awake, they went down the stairs and along the hall. At last the front door loomed before them.

171

As her fingers touched the doorknob Elizabeth noticed that her palms were damp with perspiration. She stood listening to the silence. She could hear the clock in the library ticking and Callie breathing beside her, nothing else. The darkness of the high-ceilinged hall was thick, no gleam of light pierced it. It seemed safe, but she was oddly reluctant to open the outside door. It was as if something fateful awaited her outside the house. Though she knew differently, she had the overwhelming feeling that inside the walls of Oak Shade was where their safety lay. Abruptly, impatient with her own dithering, she gave the knob a twist. Nothing happened. The door was locked!

Fumbling in the dark, she searched down the door plate to the keyhole. Then she sighed. The key was in the lock. She turned it before she had time to change her mind, wincing as it grated. As she again turned the knob the great door eased open of its own weight. She held it while Callie passed through with Joseph, and then pulled it shut after herself.

Their footsteps on the brick floor of the lower gallery made little sound as they hurried across it and down the wide steps. Avoiding the open where moonlight fell, glittering on the dew in the grass, they made for the tree-shadowed drive. Spurred by fear, they walked quickly and silently, keeping to the grass verge away from the gravel. The shadows beneath the oaks moved as the wind stirred through their branches. A rabbit or some other small creature scuttled away through the grass, and somewhere nearby a hunting owl swept by with a whir of wings. At each small sound and movement Callie made a smothered sound in the back of her throat. Now and then they would run a few steps, looking back over their shoulders at the house for signs of pursuit, probing the darkness around them with wide eyes. Callie, carrying the awkward weight of the baby, began breathing hard, and soon Elizabeth developed a stitch in her side. They slowed their pace but they could not stop.

Elizabeth's throat tightened and she averted her head as they passed the curve where two nights before she had been attacked. Once past the spot the house was no longer visible behind them and they could no longer be seen from it. They breathed easier. Elizabeth switched her bundles to the other arm and they went on.

Soon they began to catch glimpses of the chapel gleaming whitely between the trees and at last they came to the pathway that led to it. There was no sign of Darcourt, nothing to indicate that he had been there.

Looking up and down the empty drive, with its white gravel shining in the moonlight, Elizabeth considered. Were they too late? Too early? As she stood there, the night wind fluttered her skirts and cooled the film of nervous perspiration on her face. She shivered a little, wishing she had worn her shawl or her mantle.

"Dry work, walking," Callie said, her voice hushed in the still darkness.

"Yes."

"Sure am thirsty. We could have brought water if we had thought."

Elizabeth glanced at Callie. "In what?"

The woman was silent for a moment. "I could have brought the preserving jar I keep Joseph's boiled water in."

Elizabeth smiled in the dark. "Now you think of it."

Callie grunted. After a minute she spoke again. "We not the only ones leaving."

"What do you mean?"

"That Mis' Alma, she left. She packed her things and went out the back. Folks in the quarters is saying she went away with that overseer Mr. Bernard threw off the place."

"I see. So that's why she told Celestine about me. She had nothing to lose if she was leaving."

"I reckon. She sure didn't lose any sleep over that girl of hers. They say she left Mr. Bernard a letter. She told him she was going and he could see after Mis' Theresa cause she held him and his family responsible for her being the way she was. Strange, her leaving without Mr. Darcourt."

Elizabeth shook her head. "It's a terrible thing she is doing, deserting her child, even if she is unstable. But it doesn't change anything for us."

"No'm."

"I suppose we had better wait near the chapel as we were told."

"Who told us?"

"Darcourt."

Callie looked doubtfully toward the chapel just visible among the trees at the end of the path. "I don't like that place."

Neither do I, Elizabeth thought, a shiver running over her again.

"Here, give Joseph to me awhile," she said briskly.

Transferring the bundles to Callie, she took the baby in the crook of her arm and moved toward the small white building. Callie followed.

As they neared the chapel they saw a wavering light. It appeared to be inside, the glow of a candle glimmering on the marble walls, just visible through one of the double doors that stood half open. Elizabeth looked back at Callie and they quickened their steps, thinking that they were keeping Darcourt waiting inside.

With Callie crowding behind her, Elizabeth stepped through the doorway. Just inside they halted.

On the altar a single candle burned low in its socket. In the glow they saw a basket sitting on the altar bench, but there was no one there.

"Now isn't that nice and thoughtful?" Callie said. Setting her bundles on the floor she slipped past Elizabeth and reached for the checked napkin that covered the contents of the basket. "Plates and cups, cake and pie, sandwiches of some kind—little bitty things," she reported over her shoulder, and then picked up a metal flask and drew the cork.

"Smells like lemonade."

That was peculiar. It sounded very much like the refreshments Theresa had asked for that afternoon when she had wanted to prove that she could play the role of hostess. "Have some if you want it," she told Callie abstractedly, her attention caught by a sound outside. Then as she looked over her shoulder the door began to move.

The wind, she thought, or the door's own weight— Behind her the sound of lemonade gurgling from the flask into a cup halted abruptly.

"Mis' Elizabeth! The door!"

It was closing faster, and as she heard unmistakably the scrape of a footfall on the other side, she knew. They were being shut in!

She moved then, but it was too late. Even as she reached fumblingly for the edges, the thick metal door clanged to with a strength greater than her own behind it. The bolt shot home, a sharp rasp with finality in the sound, and all was silent.

CHAPTER 11

Joseph, jarred from sleep as Elizabeth ran, began to cry. She rocked him in her arms automatically as she examined the door. It was solid, cold, hard bronze. There was no inside handle to grasp or pull, no access to the locking mechanism. The hinges were on the outside and the plates with their screws were between the brick walls and the thick doors. Kneeling, Elizabeth found that she could just slip her fingers underneath the door and she called to Callie over her shoulder.

Callie gulped down the lemonade she had poured into one of the glasses provided, a kind of nervous reflex action, and hurried to help Elizabeth. But though they tugged and pulled together they could do no more than sway the doors the barest fraction of an inch.

Knowing it would do no good, they beat on them with their fists and called for help until Joseph screamed with fright. At last, exhausted, they sat down against the wall on the floor. Callie took the baby and quieted him.

"Even if one of the servants or anyone prowling about could hear us through these walls they would think we were some kind of spirits," Elizabeth said, with a kind of helpless macabre humor.

"Don't talk like that!" Callie whispered urgently, flicking a look around.

"It must be after midnight by now."

"Oh, don't—you tempting the devil!"

Elizabeth shook her head, but as she stared around at the small windows set high in the walls, the tiny altar, the bronze plaque and the chiseled letters on the crypt marker, something cold touched her heart. It would be a terrible place to die, so near the house and yet so far away. It could happen. How often did people come to the chapel? Not for months at a time. The walls were thick, the building tight and close. It was not all that far from the drive, but still a long way to make their voices heard even if they had any way of knowing when there was someone out there to hear.

In the morning they would be missed, but no one would dream of looking for them here. Darcourt, hearing they were gone, would think they had gotten away without his help and would probably keep quiet about his offer to take them into town. Was there a chance that he had not left yet? It was so late. It was possible that he might find them, though she was afraid he had already gone. Unconsciously Elizabeth crossed her fingers before she went back to her thoughts.

What an actress Theresa was. Or had her distress been an act at the time? Had she overheard her brother's words to Elizabeth and baited this trap for them? Why would she do it? Was it only dementia, or was there, somewhere in the girl's twisted brain, a reason for her actions?

"Mis' Elizabeth, I—I don't feel so good."

As Callie spoke her head lolled on her shoulders. Beads of perspiration stood out on her forehead and upper lip, while the color had drained from her face, giving it a gray cast.

"What is the matter?"

Slowly the Negro woman shook her head, and then grimaced as if that slight movement hurt her. "My—sto-

176

nach," she gasped, pressing her abdomen. "You—better take Joseph—" A cramp caught her and she heaved, closing her eyes.

Elizabeth caught the baby as he began to slip from Callie's nerveless fingers. She reached out, grabbing Callie's shoulders as she began to topple over, but she could not hold her. Callie struck the floor, drawing her legs up with a moan. Suddenly, helplessly, she began to retch.

Elizabeth was stunned by the suddenness of the sickness. Quickly she drew toward her the bundles of clothing that Callie had dropped against the wall. Opening them, she made a pallet of sorts and placed Joseph carefully upon it. Then she took one of the clean hemmed cloths that served as diapers for Joseph and tried as best she could to make Callie more comfortable. Without water it was not possible to accomplish much.

Callie, her head resting on Elizabeth's knee, raised her eyelids as if they were weighted. "That lemonade—it tasted kinda funny—bitter like. Don't you—" she licked her lips slowly as though her tongue was thick. "Don't—" she tried again to speak, her eyes wide and staring in the flickering candlelight, but she could not finish the warning. Her eyes closed and she went limp. Searching frantically, Elizabeth found a weak heartbeat, but nothing she could do roused Callie.

Was Callie right? Was there something in the lemonade? It was more than likely. What better way to insure that they did not attract attention, and help, to themselves?

Suddenly she noticed that the light in the tiny room was flickering. Looking behind her, she saw the candle guttering in its gold holder, almost out.

Joseph was asleep, Callie unconscious. She was trapped with a baby and a sick, and possibly dying, woman in that chapel of the dead. The horror of it crowded in on her in a suffocating wave, closing her throat so that she could hardly breath. It had been just bearable in the light. If the candle went out she felt that the walls of the building would close in on her and she would go screaming mad with terror.

She eased Callie's head to the floor and jumped up,

reaching for the other unlighted candle in its holder. She grasped it and held its wick to the dying flame of the other For a moment she thought it was going to catch in time then she saw the flame sinking lower and lower. It sputtered, drowning in hot wax, and then it died with a hiss But just before darkness closed in on her, her eyes were caught by something lying on the altar beside the candlestick; matches, the matches that had been used to light the candle. She knew it had to be them, because the day Grand'mere had lit the candles on the altar, the anniversary of Felix's death, she had used a candle brought from the house in a hurricane globe. And she had cleaned away every trace of dust or trash on the altar. Now there were two match stems lying there broken in three places and shaped into a circle.

Darcourt always broke his matches in just that way.

Darcourt.

As she stood there in the dark, Elizabeth began to discard her preconceived idea of Theresa as the one who had been threatening her. She did not know why it had taken her so long to do so, except that the alternative had been Bernard—

Those spiders. Could a girl like Theresa have gathered them? And placed them so cunningly under the covers without being noticed by the servants coming and going, a girl who was supposed to be semi-invalid, confined to her room? Was it really possible for her to have struck Callie and left her unconscious, a woman both taller and heavier than she? Would Theresa, so fascinated with Joseph, have left him in such obvious danger at the top of the stairs, even if she had been suddenly afraid of being discovered with him?

That night in the library, Theresa had said, "We knew you would." We. Suppose the idea had been planted deliberately in her head that Elizabeth was plotting to send her away? It would account for her rage toward her. Grand'mere had said that Theresa had always been easily led. Who could lead her better, for who could know and apply her secret fears better, than her own brother.

Then Darcourt must have sent Denise to his mother this afternoon, knowing that Alma would tell the Frenchwom-

about Elizabeth. He also must have expected, know-
g Denise and her vindictiveness toward her for usurping
r place in Grand'mere's rooms, that the woman would
t be able to resist denouncing her. He must have known
e knowledge would upset Theresa. Why would he want
do that? Why would he try to kill her and Joseph?
here had to be a reason!

Something fluttered at the back of her memory, but she
uld not quite catch it. The harder she tried, the more
usive the idea became.

A small noise made her turn. Joseph was awake again
om the sounds, waving his fists in the air and kicking his
et up, straining against the material of his long gown. He
ade a humming noise in his throat, but he did not cry.
e was so thankful that he did not, that a wave of love
r the baby swept over her and she smiled ruefully, will-
gly distracted by the thought of the things that call forth
ve.

Then, as she stood there in the dark listening to the
by, the thought came to her that unless something was
ne, Darcourt would have won. If something was not
ne, she and Joseph and Callie would die of thirst and
rvation, unless they became desperate and chose poison
a reprieve from the more lingering death. It should have
en poison for her, she had no doubt. It was unlikely that
rcourt had intended Callie to die; he had not known she
s coming. But he could not have supposed that a baby
uld drink lemonade. He had intended for Elizabeth to
, leaving Joseph to the slow, terrible death of thirst,
rvation and exposure. Alone.

Rage welled up within her at the thought, a vicious,
nding anger that had to have some outlet. Someone
uld hear her! Someone would help her! She would
ke them!

Grasping the tall gold candlestick with the burned-out
ket, she lifted it high above her head and ran at the
ined glass window near the ceiling, sending the candle-
ck smashing into the glass. She ducked as splinters of
ss rained down upon her head, and then she smashed at
gain. But even as she did it she knew it was no use. The
dow was too small for her to climb through, a slender

179

rectangle too narrow for her shoulders to pass throug[h]
and too high for her to see out of without something [o]
which to stand. Her only satisfaction was that it might [be]
easier for them to hear and to be heard.

The night breeze rushing into the opening was fresh an[d]
cool against her flushed face. She took a deep breath [to]
call for help, but then she let it out slowly. What was th[e]
use? The house was too far away for her voice to carr[y]
and no one else had any reason to be near at this hour.

What would bring someone other than a noise? A ligh[t]
a beacon, some kind of signal fire might bring them, b[ut]
she had nothing with which to light one. If she had on[ly]
watched the candle closer.

Behind her Joseph, frightened by the noise and th[e]
dark, was crying again. She could hear Callie breathi[ng]
too, in quick, shallow gasps. She leaned her head agai[nst]
the cold, pale marble of the wall. She felt so helples[s]
There should be something that she could do. She cou[ld]
not just let Joseph die here. She could not watch him di[e]
she could not stand it. Now Joseph was alone and he cou[ld]
not understand why he was on the hard pallet on the co[ld]
floor. Raising her head, she picked her way across the br[o]
ken glass to him, guiding herself by running her ha[nd]
along the wall. Picking him up in her arms, she sat dow[n]
with her back against the wall, rocking him, soothing hi[m]
At last he quieted, resting his head in the curve of h[er]
neck.

When he was quiet at last, Elizabeth sat listening to t[he]
silence around her, realizing that something was wron[g]
She strained her eyes in the blackness which was lighte[d]
only by the flow of the moonlight beyond the broken wi[n]
dow. Callie was only a dark shape against the far wall, [a]
silent shape. She had stopped breathing.

Holding the warm weight of the baby against her, Eliz[a]
beth leaned her head back, feeling the coldness of t[he]
marble striking through her clothes to her heart. The[re]
was nothing she could do for Callie. Nothing. Her ey[es]
burned, her head throbbed. The hands that held Josep[h]
trembled as she tried to straighten his gown. Deep insi[de]
her there was a growing feeling that if she made the sligh[t]

180

st sound it would turn into a scream, and so she sat very till huddled in upon herself. Soundlessly the tears rolled own her cheeks.

Her tears had dried and Joseph was once more asleep vhen she imagined she heard the noise of footsteps outide. Then came a scraping sound as a key was placed in he lock and turned. She was so stiff from sitting that she ould hardly move, but she drew back into the depths of he chapel, crouching defensively over the baby.

The door swung slowly open. A shaft of yellow lantern ight fell across the floor, silhouetting the shape of a man.

"God—" Bernard breathed.

Elizabeth stumbed to her feet, stricken dumb with a vonder laced with fear, the fear that she was terribly vrong, that Bernard had come not as a rescuer but as an xecutioner.

Then she and Joseph were in his arms being carried out nto the sweet fresh air of the night.

Bernard set Elizabeth on her feet. She looked at his ace, so grim in the light of the lantern sitting on the chap-l steps, and a little of her gladness faded.

Theresa stepped into the circle of the lantern light. "Jo-eph—is Joseph all right?" she asked fearfully.

"Yes." Elizabeth found her voice finally. "He is fine, ut I think Callie is—dead."

"How?" Bernard grated.

"Poison." Bernard's anger was chilling, and Elizabeth poke as tonelessly as possible, trying not to think of the ast hours for fear she would begin to cry. To ward off the ossibility, she spoke again. "How did you find us?"

"Theresa came to warn me that something might be going to happen to you. She brought me the key to the hapel. It had been left in her room while she slept. I lidn't recognize it at first. Denise had to tell me what it vas. I am sorry that it took so long."

Again his voice was brusque, and the thought crossed er mind that he might be trying to control some emotion, ut then she dismissed the idea. Bernard looked as if he had dressed hurriedly. He wore a shirt, without studs, pen to the waist and thrust into the waistband of his pan-

181

taloons which were in turn tucked into the top of his riding boots.

Theresa spoke up. "It wasn't Bernard's fault that w were so late. Denise would not let me see him to tell him what I wanted, not until I told her why. It was hard, th hardest thing I ever did. And when I had told her, Denise would not believe me."

"I'm surprised she ever did. What did you say to her t make her believe you, my sweet little sister?"

Darcourt spoke from the shadows at the edge of th clearing. In contrast to Bernard, he looked as if he ha dressed leisurely on arising from his bed. The white of hi dress shirt shone above the black velvet collar of his dress ing gown. On his feet he wore embroidered turkish fel slippers. In his hand was a dueling pistol with a long bar rel curving back to an ornate butt, while a second pisto hung at his side from his left hand.

Theresa started as her brother spoke, but she did no seem frightened or disturbed.

"I told her everything. I had to or she would not hav listened to me."

"It won't make any difference," he said confidently. " can always talk her around."

"Can you, Darcourt? I don't think you can, not now."

"You mean after this?" He waved the gun at the chape and Elizabeth. "There won't be anything to worry m about this, not when I am through."

"What do you mean?" Theresa asked, but from th pinched look of her features she had already guessed.

"Because they will blame it on you again," her brother told her softly, almost gently. "They will think that yo shut them up in there, and when Bernard found them yo killed them both with your brother's pistols."

"They won't! I'll tell them what happened!"

"Will they believe you? Will they, Theresa? You hav been peculiar for years, everyone knows that. Everyon knows you have been worse since Elizabeth came."

"That wasn't me, that was you! You and Denise, sh admitted she put the spiders in Elizabeth's room for you just to scare her. You lied to me about Elizabeth. She isn

182

t all like you said. She brought the baby to see me, she likes me and trusts me. If you do this I—I will tell them about our step-father. I'll tell them I saw you push him off the top of the new house during the storm! I will. I will, Darcourt!"

"By all means, tell them. But you see I have already seen to it that they half believe you had something to do with that. Do you think they will believe you when I apologize sadly for the ravings of my insane sister that I love so much, my poor darling sister?"

Elizabeth remembered again the scene in the school-room that afternoon when Denise had denounced her as an imposter. Darcourt had wanted it to happen. He had wanted to upset Theresa. It was no part of his plans that she grow better. He had needed her insane to take the blame for the murder that he had been contemplating even then.

"You are a fool if you think you can get away with it," Bernard told Darcourt in cold contempt.

"Oh, I admit it is going to seem a bit odd, that you let a young girl get the better of you. But then you always did have a soft spot for Theresa, for a foster brother. I will remind them of it. No doubt she took you unawares. But yes, I think I will get away with it. In the process I shall also get away with the better part of this estate. But you won't mind, will you, Bernard, not after we put you away in the family mausoleum behind you. I consider it poetic justice, if you can credit that." Darcourt was almost laughing, certain that he would triumph.

"I was supposed to inherit Felix's property according to the will he made before he left for Texas, but the birth of a legitimate heir nullified that. Now, with his brat dead, without heirs, that will can go into effect. And you, Bernard. Who is there to inherit your property? Grand'mere, I think, is your next of kin. It shouldn't be too hard to gain control of it from a grief-stricken old lady. If I don't have most of this estate in my own name by the time the dear old soul goes to her reward I'm not the man I think I am."

Bernard took an angry step toward him, but the muzzle of the pistol he had been holding so negligently came up.

"There is no hurry, foster-brother, but both guns are cocked and if you are impatient—?"

Elizabeth put her free hand on Bernard's arm, looking at Darcourt. "You have made a slight miscalculation, I think. You have three of us to kill and only two shots, one per gun."

"That is true, Elizabeth. But you know, I don't think I will have any difficulty snuffing out the life of one small infant once you and Bernard are dead."

"No," Theresa whispered. "No—No—No!" As her screams rose she threw herself at Darcourt, reaching for his eyes with clawing fingers.

He jerked back, the hand holding the gun going up to protect his eyes, an expression of stark disbelief on his face.

Bernard was close behind Theresa. The three grappled, struggling, twisting in the lantern light. Suddenly an explosion shattered the night as one of the pistols went off. Darcourt was thrown backward as if struck by a giant fist. Theresa shrieked, then reeled away, falling to her knees with horror printed on her face, her eyes wide and staring and her mouth soundlessly open.

Bernard threw up a hand in front of his face. In that hand he held a pistol. As the echoes of the shot died away among the trees, he walked slowly to where Darcourt lay sprawled upon the ground.

From where she stood, Elizabeth could see the great hole in Darcourt's chest that was fast turning his nightshirt black with blood. She stood watching Bernard, rocking Joseph in her arms. She did not breathe, did not relax, until she saw Bernard, his face a mask of contempt, turn his back on the figure lying so still on the ground.

CHAPTER 12

Minutes after the shot had sounded they were joined by three of the menservants Bernard had sent out to search the grounds in case they were not in the chapel. One of them was sent for the carriage. Theresa was in a state of collapse, trembling, crying, blaming herself for killing her own brother though Bernard held her against his chest and told her repeatedly that he himself had pulled the trigger. Though she accepted the support of his arms, Theresa could not seem to understand what he was saying. It was obvious that she could not walk back to the house.

Elizabeth was not at all sure that she was any better able to do so. She was not tired so much as weak, and once it had been confirmed that Callie was dead, she leaned against a tree holding Joseph to her as if for strength, waiting.

The trees around them swayed, their leaves streaming in the wind. The open door of the chapel creaked back and forth, and dried leaves scurried across the ground like live things pursued.

Elizabeth looked at Bernard trying to calm Theresa's hopeless weeping, and he glanced up as if he felt her gaze upon him. There was an inscrutable expression in his eyes that reminded her of her first impression of him. She had thought then that he would be hard to deceive, and she had been right. She had also thought that he would be slow to forgive. He had not shown a moment of concern for her. It was a frightening thing to know that this dark

Creole would be the one who would decide what was to be done with her.

Grand'mere met them at the front steps, leaning heavily on a cane. Behind her came Denise, searching among them with anxious eyes, and to one side stood Samson with a lamp in his hand.

In a few terse sentences Bernard told what had happened. When she heard that Darcourt was dead, Denise seemed to crumple, to shrink both in size and in spirit. Grand'mere had to speak to her a third time before she blinked and took charge of Theresa as the old lady commanded.

"Give me my great-grandson, and come into the house," Grand'mere said, turning away. "I think what we all need is a stimulant. Samson, brandy."

She barely looked at the butler, who inclined his head, waited until they had preceded him into the house, and then went to do her bidding as quickly as his dignity permitted.

Grand'mere led the way into the library. In the light of three lamps, she examined Joseph to be sure he had taken no injury. The brandy decanter and glasses were brought on a silver tray, and then Samson departed silently, pulling the door closed behind him.

"Though ladies ordinarily do not take spirits, my nerves have been sadly shattered since I discovered Joseph gone from his bed. I'm sure you must be quite done up, too, Elizabeth." Grand'mere took a small sip from the glass Bernard handed her.

Elizabeth followed suit but did not answer, letting a stiff smile suffice.

"How you came to do such a bird-witted thing I don't know. It was quite unnecessary and not at all in line with your usual common sense."

When Elizabeth, looking into her brandy glass and watching the liquor swirl in its depths, still said nothing, Grand'mere turned to Bernard.

"Is it true? Did the child shoot her brother as she keeps saying? It seems unlikely. She has always been abjectly fond of him."

"I killed him. At least, that is what Theresa must be
186

nade to believe. To be perfectly truthful, I don't know who pulled the trigger, it may even have been Darcourt himself, but Theresa must never be allowed to think that she is responsible."

"Is that supposed to help? I know you feel that she was showing a marked improvement the last two days, but after all, what chance is there now that she will ever live normally, when her brother has died violently before her eyes and her mother deserted her?"

Bernard rubbed his eyes. "We will see. It is possible that now she is free of Darcourt's influence she will improve. We know now what happened to make her as she was." He told his grandmother what Theresa had said, that she had seen Darcourt kill Gaspard.

"My poor Gaspard. Who would have thought that Darcourt could have managed it?"

Bernard tossed off the rest of his brandy and set the glass down. "We all tend to think of people who will not turn their hands to anything, who prefer to loaf through life, as being somehow unintelligent, of being as lazy of mind as they are of body. It isn't so. Darcourt would never do his share here at the plantation because he felt that we owed him something, that he had been cheated under our father's will. He thought he should have been given at least one of the plantations that make up the estate. I have always known that he felt that way. I don't know, maybe he was right."

"Nonsense. Darcourt was not Gaspard's child. It may be that my son recognized the instability in his foster children. In any case, Darcourt had an inheritance from his own father, and Alma let it run through her hands while he was still in short pants, long before she married your father."

"That was hardly Darcourt's fault."

"You would excuse him? The man who murdered your father and tried to murder you and Elizabeth as well as my great-grandson?"

"Darcourt thought he had been slighted. Apparently Felix, who was much more of a brother to Darcourt than I since they had more in common, felt so too. He made out his will in Darcourt's favor before he went to Texas. I

187

knew the circumstances. I blame myself for the things tha have happened. I should have realized that Darcourt wa behind it, but poor Theresa never denied that she was re sponsible for the things that were happening when she wa asked. Heaven alone knows what Darcourt told her to ac count for them and obtain her cooperation. He was alway full of schemes to make a quick fortune and take Theres and her mother away, perhaps that was it. Anyway, I'r sure Felix never expected to be killed, and in truth, I hav trouble picturing Felix originating the idea of the will.

"It was Alma who talked him into it. She told me. Elizabeth corrected him.

"Sweet Alma," Grand'mere said dryly. "I imagine sh will get what she deserves with that man. But to get bac to what you were saying?"

"Legal technicalities due to the manner and place of h death held up the disposition of Felix's estate, and then w learned that there would be an heir who naturally take precedence under our laws. Darcourt must have bee livid, to be cheated out of his fortune again. No doubt h felt justified, but it takes a strange sort of mind to contem plate killing a child."

Grand'mere stared before her, her face hard, thoug there was an expression of sadness around the eyes.

"Elizabeth, though she was not Joseph's mother, wa his next of kin, next in line of succession to the inher tance, so naturally she had to die also. With the dire heirs dead then I imagine Darcourt thought that I could b persuaded to honor the intent of Felix's first will. Or alter nately, you Grand'mere, after I arrived on the scene t spoil things for him. He was always slighting the Creol conception of honor but he was always quick to take ad vantage of it."

"No doubt you are right, *mon cher*," Grand'mere saic nodding. "I suppose we must make an effort to inforr Alma of the fate of her son?"

"I will see to it. I doubt she will be very surprised. can't picture her leaving without him, unless she had dis covered that he was behind the incidents, and that he wa planning something desperate."

Joseph, tiring of the inactivity of lying on his back o

he black silk of Grand'mere's lap, and beginning to be hungry, started to fret.

"Oh, dear. It is a great pity about Callie. I had quite grown to like her, an excellent woman. You were quite right to take up the cudgel in her defense, *chère*. I think you will find that it was arsenic that killed her. I have been afraid of something dreadful happening ever since that ninny, Alma, started to use it."

"It seems likely," Bernard agreed, without giving Elizabeth a chance to speak.

Grand'mere went on. "We must find some way of feeding our little man until a new wet nurse can be found. I had better send to the quarters in the morning." She gathered the baby against her shoulder, patting his back ineffectually.

"I think you will have to act sooner than that," Bernard said, a smile curving the austere line of his mouth as Joseph howled.

"Yes," Grand'mere said, distracted in her concern as she got up and went toward the door. "I will have to send Samson immediately; where has he got off to? Hush, hush, my sweet, it can't be helped. Perhaps a cookie—"

She trailed off, moving toward the door. Elizabeth went quickly to help her.

"No, no. That is quite all right. I can manage. Besides, I believe Bernard wants a few words with you. I tried to tell you earlier tonight, but you put me off until morning. Well, never mind. Perhaps it will come better from him. Tact was never my strong point."

The door closed behind her and she could be heard speaking to Samson in the hall.

Elizabeth had been able to find little hope that Bernard would relent and allow her to stay. After Grand'mere's rather strange statement she could find none. She drank her brandy for courage, suppressing a reflex cough. Then she sat toying with her glass, watching Bernard covertly and wondering if he was trying to find the best words to use to tell her to leave.

He reached over and took the glass from her nerveless fingers and set it behind him on the desk.

"I am sorry for what happened tonight, sorry that it

189

could have taken place on property belonging to me. I wish I could have foreseen and prevented it."

"It wasn't your fault."

"No. It wasn't," he took her up abruptly. "If you had not tried to run away from me it would never have happened!"

"I was not running away from you," Elizabeth protested.

"Weren't you?" His smile was grim. "I owe you another apology for the manner in which I treated you this afternoon. It was not realistic to expect you to be completely honest with me. Nor was it my place to mete out punishment for my disappointment."

"Don't. Please. I should be apologizing to you. I should never have come here as I did. I wouldn't have, except that I wanted Joseph to have his heritage, to grow up as part of his father's tradition, and because I couldn't keep him as well as you would be able to do. It wasn't the money. Truly it wasn't. I'm sorry. I will try to make it up to you, all of you, if you will allow me to stay. Not as Felix's widow, of course, but as Joseph's aunt."

"That is impossible." Bernard turned away from her, fidgeting with the cigar box on the desk.

After lowering her pride enough to make the appeal she had sworn she would never make, his harsh refusal sent tears crowding into her throat. They were not simply tears of disappointment or even of regret for the loss of Joseph. There was some deeper feeling hidden behind them, a feeling she would not analyze, not now. She could hardly speak as she asked, "Why?"

"It would be intolerable."

Slow to forgive? She had been wrong. He would never forgive her.

"I—I understand."

He swung around, his eyes narrowed. "No. I don't think you do. It would be intolerable—it has been intolerable to have you constantly near, and yet never be able to speak to you as a man, never be able to touch you because of that shroud of widow's weeds you wear. I could not smile at you or even make you laugh as I wanted to, out of respect for my dead brother. No, I will not tolerate that again. Jo-

ph's aunt? I swear by all I hold most dear that the only
ay you will stay in this house is as my wife. If you will
t do that then you can go!"

"Your wife!" Her green eyes, glittering with unshed
ars, were wide. "But what of Celestine?"

"What of her?"

"She expects to marry you."

"Celestine will be leaving us in the morning. It seems
e was not at all pleased with the way she was treated this
ternoon, or with the way her information was received.
s for marrying her, I told her as politely as I was able
at I did not care to have an informer as my wife."

"What did she say?" Elizabeth allowed a small smile to
ach her eyes.

"A great deal, but the pertinent thing was to accuse me
preferring an imposter."

A thought struck Elizabeth as she remembered the sly
ings that Darcourt had said, the poison that he had given
r so much more effectively in words than he had man-
ed to do in lemonade. She said uncertainly, "Not for the
oney—?"

"What money?" Bernard looked genuinely puzzled.

"That Felix—"

"My darling idiot. Since you were never Felix's wife
u are not entitled to the money and it goes back into Jo-
ph's estate whether I marry you or not, but I certainly
ve no intention of marrying you for a paltry sum like
at."

"Oh." Elizabeth blushed. "I was forgetting. I have
own so used to thinking of it as mine."

At that he laughed and drew her into his arms. "Then
ll you listen while I tell you I love you? And will you be-
ve me?"

"I'm not sure. You have acted at times as if you hated
."

"Love often masquerades as hate," he told her softly,
ut I will enjoy convincing you that I speak the truth."

At last she raised her head from his shoulder.

"What will we tell them, all those people who have
ard of me through the plantation grapevine as Ellen, Fe-
's widow?"

191

"We will introduce you to them as Elizabeth, my wife
His mouth took on a bitter twist. "The events of this d
will provide gossip for the parish for a long time to com
I will wager anything you wish that in the gossip over Da
court's death, and then our approaching marriage, no o
will notice a change of name." Then he smiled down
her again as if dismissing all thoughts of that nature. '
they should notice they will either think you were chr
tened with several names, as they were, or that they m
have heard it wrong. It doesn't matter very much to r
what they think."

"And if someone should question me about it?"

"Smile and look innocent as you so well know how
do."

"Suppose they ask you?"

"They won't," he said, and looking at his face th
could be so forbidding, Elizabeth knew that he spo
nothing but the truth.

He smiled, looking down at her, and the smile eras
the sternness, touched his eyes with tenderness, and so
tened the hard lines of his lips that he lowered to he
expecting her surrender.

There are many things more important to a woman
heart than winning a battle of wills. He was not disa
pointed.